Jim Scheers

THIS IS WHAT YOU WANT, THIS IS WHAT YOU GET

A Novel

Paul –
Enjoy!
Jim Sche

Northampton House Press

THIS IS WHAT YOU WANT, THIS IS WHAT YOU GET. © 2015 by Jim Scheers. All rights reserved, including the right to reproduce this book, or portions thereof, in any form.

Cover Design: Naia Poyer, from a photo from stock.xchng by Ruben G.S., with thanks.

First ebook edition, Northampton House LLC, 2014 . ISBN . 978-1-937997-44-1.

Northampton House Press print first edition, 2015, ISBN . 978-1-937997-51-9 .

Library of Congress Control Number: 2014946870

10 9 8 7 6 5 4 3 2.

THIS IS WHAT YOU WANT, THIS IS WHAT YOU GET

A SIDE

April-June 1987

The individual cannot become human by himself. . . . Isolated or self-isolated Being remains mere potentiality or disappears into nothingness.

—Karl Jaspers, *Existenzphilosophie*

1

THRASH

The building squatted in the shadows at the end of an unlit gravel lot. A wide concrete box with pock-marked walls streaked gray and black like a newspaper left in the rain. Nick slowed as he drove past. Was this the place or not? There was no sign. Only a floodlight over the front door. The rest of the block was darkened, abandoned warehouses with shattered windows. At least here headlights and silhouettes of people were moving around, so he pulled in, his car lurching through the lot's deep craters.

On the way to the entrance, broad-shouldered boys with shaved heads stood with boots planted far apart, drinking from beer bottles hidden inside flight jackets, their jeans rolled up to the top of tall black combat boots. Their gazes passed over Nick. He kept his head down. He didn't like people looking at him. He wasn't used to it and was never sure what they saw.

Two girls leaned against the wall beside the battered front door, passing a cigarette between them. They were both white-faced, with dark hair hanging like melting tar. One asked Nick for a dollar to get inside. Black eye shadow ringed her eyes like a burglar's mask. He shook his head, then opened the door.

At the end of a short hallway two large men sat on stools on either side of wooden double doors. "What the fuck is this?" one said.

They both got up and blocked his path. Their shoulders seemed to span the entire width of the hall. Beneath leather jackets they wore matching orange t-shirts. One bouncer had a dark, wiry beard. The other wore a white bandanna pulled down to his eyebrows.

"You here for the show?"

Nick looked down at a crack in the concrete floor. "Yeah."

"Know where you are?"

"The 321 Club?"

He couldn't keep his voice from inflecting into a question. But this had to be the place. Every other street he'd driven down was either crumbling factories or tiny row homes with bars over their windows.

The bouncer cocked his head back, chin raised so he could look down at Nick. "You sure?"

"Yes."

"Know who's playing tonight?"

"Dag Nasty and the Circle Jerks," Nick said.

"Hardcore, right?"

Was the bouncer asking or telling him? Nick wasn't sure. He listened to the college stations all the time now, and heard the DJs say "hardcore" sometimes. But he didn't know which bands were hardcore and which weren't. Didn't know anybody else who liked this music. Didn't even know what Dag Nasty or the Circle Jerks looked like, or what to expect inside. But he was tired of taping songs off the tiny clock radio in his bedroom and scrounging the mall record store bins and finding nothing. He wanted more, so he'd listened for the DJs to announce the upcoming shows, and checked the newspapers. In this part of New Jersey, this club was the only place to go.

"Yeah." He tried to meet the bouncers' squinting glare. "Hardcore."

"Like you'd know."

Nick was surprised to feel a small, hard kernel of anger forming inside his chest.

"Uh oh." The bouncer with the bandanna looked over at the other man. "He's getting pissed now."

The bearded man laughed. "Put your hands up, ace," he said to

Nick.

"What?"

"Put your fucking hands up."

He lifted his arms and the man patted down his jacket, then his legs. He tried not to fidget. The alcove smelled dank and sour, like an old stone cellar.

"All right," the bouncer said. "Get the fuck out of here."

"Huh?"

He wasn't sure if they were letting him in or kicking him out. Somebody else had come in and now stood close behind him. A scrawny young man with a shaved head, an unlit cigarette in his mouth.

"*Huh?*" the bouncer mimicked. "You're here for the show, right? Drove from the suburbs to Trenton for this shit, right?" He kicked open the inner door. "So go ahead, ace!"

"Watch that face," the other bouncer said. "Cover up."

Inside was a wooden counter with a rusty cash register. A black man leaned over the countertop and peered into the alcove. "Stop kicking the door!" he shouted.

The bouncers pointed at Nick. "It wasn't us. It was him."

"I didn't do anything," Nick said quickly.

"Shit." The man laughed. He had a lean face, his sunken nose pushed to one side. "Don't jump. It's ten dollars, chief." He pointed at Nick and said to the bouncers, "You check him out?"

"Who? The face? Yeah, he's cool."

The young skinhead bowed his head and, hands in pockets, tried to slide past Nick. The bouncer grabbed him by the neck and pulled him back into the alcove. "Where you going, asshole?"

Nick gave the man at the cash register ten dollars and walked down another hallway. Over the PA system came a loping guitar riff. A nasal, juvenile voice whined *when I went to your schools, I went to your churches?* Nick recognized the band. Suicidal Tendencies. The knot in his stomach loosened a little.

The walls were black. Beneath a cloud of cigarette smoke people leaned on a long U-shaped bar. There were only a few stools. To the right, wooden tables and chairs, and a wide dance floor in front of a narrow stage. To the left, a long dark corridor with more bouncers, arms crossed, at the end. Nick went around to the back of the bar where it was less crowded. A short, round, bespectacled guy in a flannel shirt perched at the end, bent over a paperback. He squinted up at Nick, then went back to his book.

The bartender was young and fresh-faced, with short spiked hair. "I can't comp you," he told Nick.

"Excuse me?"

The bartender looked confused. "You're not with the band?"

"No. You think I'm in a band?"

"Well, we had an opening band that was all these college kids. They got chased off stage."

He lowered his head. "Not me."

"I didn't think they'd be coming back. What can I get you?"

Nick ordered a Coke, uncomfortably aware of his appearance. Baggy jeans, black sneakers, a worn gray t-shirt and his father's old army field jacket. His black hair combed back in an offhand way, stray strands sticking out over his ears and spilling over his collar.

He fidgeted with his plastic cup. The crowd lining the bar was mixed. Skinny, dark-haired girls in white makeup and long black dresses. Shirtless skinheads, wearing jeans with suspenders hanging down. Young men with mohawks or spiked hair. Hardcore played over the PA like continuously rolling thunder: fast crashing guitars and bellowing choruses. A small crowd was forming in front of the stage, some of the men hopping up and down in place. The lights were low except for a white spot on the crew working on stage.

He took a sip of Coke, put it down, slid it around, took another sip. Along the bar people were shouting to each other, waving down the bartender. He tried not to stare. All those times alone in his bedroom with the cassette player, swapping out tapes, or driving around at night, flicking between WTSR and WPRB, he'd never been able to picture who else was listening.

The slicing opening chords of "Let's Lynch the Landlord" came on over the PA. Some of the people at the bar bobbed their heads in time with the music. The guy with the paperback beat a fist on the bartop, never looking up from his book. In front of the stage people were dancing now, swinging their arms, shoving each other. Nick craned his neck to get a better view. Did he look like that in his room, bouncing around to the same music?

The song ended and the PA went silent. The crowd turned

towards the DJ booth set back in the corner and booed.

"Oh stop it," the DJ said. "Dag Nasty's coming on soon."

The crowd in front of the stage grew larger. Fewer and fewer ringed the bar. Nick stepped sideways to get a better view and tripped over someone's legs.

"Hey!" a girl shouted. "Walk much?"

"Excuse me!" another said. "People down here!"

Three girls sitting huddled close together on the footrest beneath the bar all glared up at him.

"Sorry," he said.

The one he'd tripped over was petite, with a childlike face, dressed in jeans and a denim jacket covered in pins with logos of different bands. Her blonde hair stood in inch-high barbs along the top of her head. She turned to her friends. "He said 'sorry.'"

The others wore long black dresses. Thick silver chains hung from their necks and wrists. The skinny one brushed brown hair back from her face. "That was nice."

The third girl was bigger than the others, with broad shoulders and bleached white hair gathered in long plumes at the top of her head. She took a drag on a cigarette, gaze fixed on Nick. She had the saddest, palest eyes he'd ever seen.

"Why are you under the bar?" he asked the small blonde girl.

She turned to her friends. "He wants to know why we're under the bar."

"We're hiding," the dark-haired girl said without looking up.

"From what?"

"He wants to know what we're hiding from," the blonde girl said. She reached over, took the cigarette from the tall girl and put it in her mouth.

"From you!" the dark-haired girl said to Nick. Her white makeup made her look like a marble statue. "We're hiding from you."

"Yeah!" The small blonde blew a column of smoke. "So stop following us, you crazy psycho."

The tall girl shook her head. "You guys . . ."

He stepped away. "I'm going to go watch the band."

"He's going to go watch the band now," the short girl said.

"Tell him to have fun."

"'Bye," the tall one said. Even smiling, she still looked sad.

He stood in the back of the crowd. The floor in front of the stage was a checkerboard of black and white linoleum covered in bootprints. People slipped past, pressing forward. He'd stepped in something sticky—spilled soda, probably—and whenever he shifted his feet, the soles of his sneakers peeled away with a sound like a zipper opening. He decided to stay where he was.

Four skinny men in jeans and baggy t-shirts sauntered across the stage. Two slung on guitars and plugged them in. A few random notes sounded. The stage lights flashed on and the crowd cheered and clapped. The band was young, maybe twenty, twenty-one—not much older than Nick—but they looked exhausted. Faces gray, dark circles under their eyes.

The crowd shifted, pushing forward. Everything was dark beneath the low cloud of cigarette smoke. The guitar ripped out a few quick notes, and then the drums and bass collided like a car skidding out of control. The singer, eyes wide, braced one foot on the monitor at the edge of the stage and leaned out over the outstretched hands and raised fists. He half-screamed, half-sang, *"How can I say I'm really free? How can I say I'm really me?"*

The band jumped and twisted across the stage as if wrestling with their guitars. The crowd surged in waves, crashing up against the foot of the stage, then rolling back. Between verses the singer straightened, hands at his sides, mouth hanging open. But when he sang he crouched low and hunched forward, forcing the words from his lungs.

Nick stood transfixed and silent throughout the entire set, the drums thumping in his chest, the bass pounding underneath his feet. But in his mind he screamed along with every line of every song. He hardly noticed the swirling chaos in front of the stage, the arms and fists flying, the bouncers wading into the crowd and dragging people out in headlocks.

"This is our last song," the singer said, his t-shirt dark and sagging with sweat. "It's called 'Justification.' This goes out to the guy that just called us pussies."

The guitarist struck the same chord four times, pausing between each stroke, head bobbing. The drums and bass thudded quickly beneath the whine of feedback. The singer cast his head back and roared the first verse. The crowd shuddered. Halfway through the song, the singer leapt into the audience. They closed around him. Nick was carried forward in the press of people.

The microphone popped up in the air. Someone grabbed it and howled so loudly the speakers on stage crackled with static. That guy passed it to someone else who shouted the next verse. The singer had disappeared. The microphone was passed around again. A girl sang next. What sounded like a little kid shouted, "Skinheads suck!" Someone growled, someone sang a whole verse, someone else screamed the next line. As Nick braced against the back of the fat kid in front of him, trying to create a space in the heat and crush of people, the microphone dropped into his hands. He stared at the ball of silver mesh. It was heavier than he'd thought it would be.

He opened his mouth but no sound came out.

The fat kid turned and snatched it from him. In a nasal bellow, he finished the rest of the song. The band struck the last note.

The bass player stepped up to his microphone. "Somebody want to pass our singer back to the front, please?"

Nick turned away, eyes downcast, and immediately stumbled into people standing close behind him. The girls from under the bar, without their tall friend.

The dark-haired one turned to the small blonde. "He keeps getting in our way."

"I *know*," she replied in a feigned Valley girl voice. "He's like *totally* stalking us."

Nick apologized and moved around them. He tried to get to the bar but the crowd was already two rows deep. He waited. *You've lost the truth that used to live inside of you.* The last line of that song. Which he had known. If he ever got the microphone again, he would scream it as loud as he could.

After a long wait, the bartender said, "Another Coke?"

"I couldn't get a drink, could I?"

"The real bar's in the back. You got ID?"

"No."

"Don't even try. It's the Berlin Wall back there."

"All right."

"Another Coke?"

"No." He looked back at the stage. "I'm going up front."

The bartender nodded. "It's gonna be a hell of a pit."

Nick worked his way back into the crowd. All around him people were shifting their feet. No one spoke. A man to his left dropped a cigarette to the floor and stomped it out. Nick didn't see too many people here by themselves. He wondered if he should've brought someone with him, but he had only a few friends left from high school, and they only talked when somebody's parents had gone away and they could get drunk in a basement. Nick's parents never took vacations, so he didn't get many calls now. That was fine. He had less and less to say to his old friends anyway.

He looked around, but didn't see the girls from under the bar. Had they been mocking him or flirting? The dark-haired one looked like a skeleton, but the short blonde had a round, girlish face that contrasted strangely with the barbed-wire haircut. He dismissed the thought of seriously trying to talk to them. Together they had this weird impenetrable defense, like a forcefield encircling them. Not the snottiness of the preppy girls he'd known in high school, or the lazy sarcasm of the women in the office. No, it was more like the wariness of a small, wild animal, the way they watched his face, as if looking for the sign to attack or flee.

Without any announcement, the Circle Jerks came out on stage and picked up their guitars. The singer bounced on the balls of his feet like a boxer. He was small and wiry and topped with a mane of curly brown hair. The guitarist ground out fast, jagged notes. The bass and drums kicked in. The music quickened. The singer bent over and snarled *"You yell out in defiance, you're backed up against the wall."* All around Nick the shadows of the crowd shook, shoulders rocking, heads snapping back and forth.

The band launched into the next song without a break. The crowd tightened and started pushing backwards. Nick inhaled the smell of sweat and cigarettes. Someone bumped him from behind and then crossed in front of him. A broad-shouldered man with slicked-back bleached-blond hair. On the back of his leather jacket was a skull with a mohawk and in hand-painted white letters PUNK'S NOT DEAD. The man tried to press forward but a wall of people had formed in front of them, all packed close together. Nick could only see part of the stage past the man's head, so he angled closer.

Something was happening up front. The wall of people kept moving back. The man in the leather jacket stumbled into Nick, braced a hand on his shoulder, and pushed off into the crowd, clearing a space. The song stopped. The crowd cheered. Nick followed in the blonde guy's path and slid up alongside him. The wall of people had formed a circle in front of the stage and Nick was now part of it.

Young men inside the circle paced back and forth across the scuffed checkerboard dance floor. The sweat streaming down their bare backs glistened in the stage lights. One with a shaved head faced the audience, his back to the stage. Combat boots laced almost to his knees, a flannel shirt tied around his waist. His body was all ribs and bony shoulder blades. He glared at the crowd and grinned without parting his lips, bobbing his head as if the music were still playing.

Barrel-chested bouncers stood around the circle, arms folded. One shook his head and sneered.

The band launched into "Coup d'Etat." The skinhead jumped into the air, fists flying in wild arcs. Everyone in the circle started strutting and kicking and punching the air. People leapt in, were pushed across, fell down, got yanked to their feet and then thrown back across. The band never paused. One song went right into the next. Sometimes it sounded like they were playing two at once. All around Nick people pumped their fists and jumped up and down. No one ever stopped moving, the band never stopped playing, the band and the crowd drenched in sweat and gulping for air.

Towards the end of "Killing for Jesus," the lights flickered on and off. People who knew the song folded their hands and bowed their heads in mock prayer as the singer bellowed "*'cause I'm never bored . . . when I'm killing for the Lord . . .*"

The lights flickered again and the DJ came on over the PA. "Sorry, folks. Time to close out. The local authorities say we have to shut it down by ten."

Groans and curses rose from the crowd. The whole band flashed the DJ the finger and stalked off the stage. The crowd stomped their feet in unison and screamed for an encore.

"No encore. It's ten, folks. They'll shut us down."

A few headed for the doors. The rest continued stomping.

A tiny girl with green hair next to Nick shouted, "Fuck you! We're not leaving!"

The Circle Jerks walked back onstage. The singer raised his index finger towards the DJ booth and the band picked up their guitars.

"He thinks we're just gonna do one song," the singer said to the crowd.

The drummer counted off and the band tore into "Wasted." The circle opened in a swirl of flailing arms and legs. Bodies flew past Nick in a blur. Fists prodded his back. He bent his knees, clenched his jaw and leapt in. He tried to swing his arms and strut the way the other guys were but somebody collided with him and he fell face down. Someone landed on his back, knocking the air out of his lungs. Hands pressed the back of his head, then pushed off.

"Pick him up! Pick him up!" somebody shouted. Fingers grasped the back of his jacket and yanked him to his feet. It was the older guy with the PUNK'S NOT DEAD jacket.

"Thanks," Nick gasped.

"You're all right," the guy said, then he put his palms on Nick's chest and shoved him back into the pit. He stumbled into the path of a lanky skinhead. Their feet entangled and they both collapsed to the floor. The skinhead growled, "Fuck!"

The song ended. "Sorry," Nick said.

The skinhead pulled him to his feet. He slapped him in the back of the head. "Whatever."

"That's it," the DJ said. "Let's go before they shut us down."

The singer looked back at the band. The drummer counted off and they launched into "Firebaugh."

The crowd charged the stage. The skinhead next to Nick leapt up and surfed across upraised hands towards the band. The singer bowed down and sang right into his face. The lights flickered on and off. The crowd bounced up and down in place, everyone clutching each other's shoulders.

Over the PA, the DJ said, "That's it. We're shutting it down."

The Circle Jerks kept playing. The singer whipped his body back and forth, throwing off sweat like rain, long hair flying. Nick's pulse throbbed in his head; his entire body was a wire stretched tight. The crowd opened into a circle again, everyone stomping and flailing. He leapt in, hips swinging, knees up, feet kicking. He didn't fall down this time.

The stage lights turned off but the band kept playing in the dark. The bouncers grabbed people at random and dragged them to the door. The overhead lights went on and suddenly all the faces were visible. Flushed, shining with sweat, mouths hanging open. An illuminated cloud of cigarette smoke swirled above their heads. With a hiss of static, the music cut out.

But the crowd kept going, thrashing in the white glare of the lights. No music. Only quick panting breaths. Grunts and curses when bodies collided. Combat boots stomping across the floor.

Outside, it was starting to rain. Nick lingered in the parking lot with the rest of the crowd. The Circle Jerks were loading equipment into a van pulled up to the side door. One man held a big towel over their heads. Nick's back ached. His knees were shaking. Raindrops pelted his face. He didn't want to go home but felt stupid just standing there. People wandered the lot, talking and laughing. They all seemed to know each other.

A chain-link fence surrounded the entire place. Beyond it police cars with headlights on lined the curb. No streetlamps, only the single bright floodlight above the door. The smudged gray walls of the club seemed to be flaking away like dead skin. Then Nick realized it was tattered flyers, pasted one atop the other, all wrinkled and molting.

A voice behind him said, "Hi."

The tall girl from the bar, the one with sad blue eyes. She had a long black coat wrapped around her shoulders and a cigarette cupped in one hand. "You look like you lost your home." She cocked her head and exhaled a plume of smoke out the side of her mouth.

"I have a home." Nick said.

"Where?"

"Hopewell."

"Never heard of it."

"Nobody has."

She smiled, eyes fixed on his face. "How old are you?"

"Nineteen. You?"

"Eighteen."

He wasn't sure he believed her. The languid way she smoked, the steady way she gazed, made him think she was much older. But she had a smooth face and a childish habit of biting her lower lip.

She said, "Can I ask you something else?"

Around the parking lot car engines turned over and headlights flicked on.

"Sure."

Headlights shone on her pale face. "You ever think about death?"

He felt an empty space open in front of him, as if he'd tripped but not yet hit the ground. She waited for him to answer.

"Yeah."

"You know what I'm talking about, right?" Her eyebrows arched.

"Yeah. I do."

"I thought so." She placed a hand on his chest and kissed him lightly on the cheek. "My name's Victoria."

The bouncers came outside and shined their flashlights on the people in the lot. "Everybody get the hell out of here or we'll have the cops escort you out."

The girl, Victoria, didn't move, only blinked against the rain. "Are you going to the Descendants show next Sunday?"

"I don't know."

"I'll look for you."

A flashlight's beam glanced across Nick's eyes and he winced.

"You two," the bouncer said. "Get moving."

Nick turned to leave. "Maybe I'll see you there." He paused and looked over his shoulder. She was watching him walk away. Her huge black trench coat hung down to the toes of her boots. She crossed her arms and pulled the coat around her, shoulders hunched forward as if she were bracing against a strong wind.

Driving home, Nick played the radio low to subdue the buzzing in his ears. It only took a few minutes to find Route 31, which led out of Trenton and past the dormant supermarkets and office parks of Ewing and Pennington. He took the exit for Hopewell, headlights guiding the way down the curving, tree-shrouded back roads. No other cars, even though it was only 10:30. Just a few deer, blinking and tentative, along the roadside.

Lights glowed in the living room, but all the other windows were dark. His mother would be asleep upstairs. His father on the sofa, struggling to stay awake in front of the TV. Nick quietly shut the door of his car. He didn't want to look at anyone or even speak. He felt different, changed. But if he walked into the house right now he'd snap back into who he was before. He felt like a fugitive, like a thief who'd stolen something secret and precious. He wanted to hang onto that feeling a little bit longer.

He circled around to the back, where a creek ran across the far edge of the lawn and through the backyards of his neighbors. He walked along it, heading for the center of town. He walked through here often, late at night, staying in the shadows beneath the trees, avoiding the squares of light the houses cast on the lawns, glancing in windows as he passed, to see a living room flickering blue in the light of a television, or a gray-haired woman leaning over a kitchen sink determinedly scrubbing a big pot, or a young woman in sweats cradling a crying baby and staring up at the ceiling. It reminded him of the museum his parents took him to up in New York when he was little: stuffed animals in reproductions of their natural habitats, frozen in stiff poses behind panes of glass.

He flipped up the collar of his army jacket. The rain had let up, but water dripped off the branches of the trees as he brushed past. The creek led to a grove of trees, then a narrow path that brought him to the center of town, with its one strip mall of a few small shops and a lone traffic light. Just off the main street sat an abandoned office building, a faded two-story with a small cracked parking lot in front. On the first floor was a narrow alcove beneath an overhang. Nick sat down on the bench tucked inside it, the damp wooden slats creaking. He crossed his arms against the night chill. Beneath the lone streetlight the wet asphalt glimmered like a reptile's skin. His ears were still ringing. He leaned back, wincing as his sore ribs pressed against the back of the bench. He touched the spot on his chest where the girl had placed her hand.

Do you ever think about death?

For the longest time, through junior high and most of high school, the thought had been there. Eventually, after several therapists and psychologists, he'd learned—not how to face or even talk about it— but how to smother it. He'd finally figured out what everyone wanted to hear. So then he could say all the right things, do what he was supposed to do, create an airtight disguise of normalcy.

Eventually, it was like he'd erased the thought. But in its absence, there was this cavern left behind that made all his other thoughts— about work and his parents and girls who never called him back and friends who'd slipped away— mere echoes in that big empty space. If he only knew how to put all that into words, that was what he would've said to the girl.

But maybe she already knew. Just to ask meant she saw something, simply by looking at him. But how? What had she seen?

Wincing, he rose. Work tomorrow. He felt heavy and tired just thinking about it. He bounced on the balls of his feet the way that one singer had, still hearing the drums and guitars, the screaming, in his head. He looked around. The lights were off in the houses across the street. He swung his arms, trying to remember how the guys had strutted and flailed around the pit. It wasn't that hard. Just move the way the music sounded. He hunched forward, swinging his fists and lifting his knees, moving in a circle around the parking lot, sneakers scuffing the wet pavement, singing under his breath. *"And I can't believe it's true, you've lost the truth that used to live inside of you."*

2

WHAT WAS MISSED

Monday morning, Nick pulled his tiny Chevy Chevette into the sprawling lot of the ADR Corporation, blasting a mix tape, Dag Nasty shaping a bubble of sound and rhythm to insulate him from the day's pending monotony, so that even after he got out he kept the song going in his head, checking his reflection in the car window and tucking in the button-down shirt he'd left untucked in his rush to get out the door, hurrying through the side entrance past the security guards at the desk sipping from styrofoam coffee cups, down the long carpeted hallways past the Customer Service department deaf to the hushed voices coming from cubicles, stopping off at the cafeteria to toss his bag lunch into the refrigerator, then down the steps to the Finance department and its oddly empty cubicles.

Deborah, his boss, stood by the printer in the center of the department, pulling a page at a time as they came out. "Morning," she said.

"Hi."

She frowned. "On break already?"

"What?" Nick froze just outside his cubicle.

She glanced down at his jacket. "You're just getting in?" She rolled her eyes. "That's just great . . ."

He took off his jacket, sat down in the cubicle and scanned his desk for some clue to his offense. Nothing. Just the same stacks of invoices from the week before and an empty coffee cup.

Deborah came to stand in the entrance of his cubicle. A thin woman in her thirties with short black hair feathered back over her ears. Lately she'd started wearing shiny suits with shoulder pads as wide as doorways. She teetered forward on high heels like a diver at the edge of a spring board. "Why aren't you in class?"

He wheeled his chair back, realizing only then the whole department was silent. No calculator tapes whirring. No voices. "I, uh . . ."

"You forgot."

"No." He struggled to remember what had happened last week. Had there been some announcement?

"I don't believe it." She shook her head. "Maybe if you hurry, you can catch the second half."

He quickly paged through the papers in his inbox but found only more invoices.

"You're checking your *mail*? Right now?"

"I had to get some invoices out of the way," he said. "They were really important rush jobs."

"That's great, Nick. Just great." She walked away.

He grabbed a pen and jumped up. "I'm going right now," he called as she slammed the door to her office. He zipped down the aisle of cubicles, skinny wool knit tie swinging like a short leash someone had lost hold of. He turned right, heading towards the stairs at the end of a long corridor. His department was on the bottom floor of a four-story corporate building. The meeting or whatever it was would probably be on the second or third floor where the conference rooms were. He peered into offices as he passed. He rarely spoke to anyone at work, so hardly anyone knew him. He couldn't just poke his head into somebody's office and ask where this thing was.

One of the accounting managers strolled down the hall, heading his way. Tortoiseshell eyeglasses, dress shirt and silk tie, slacks with suspenders. He stared at a point somewhere over Nick's shoulder.

Nick cleared his throat. "Excuse me . . . Bill?"

"I'm Rich," the man said with a reluctant glance over one

shoulder.

"Right. Rich. Sorry. I was wondering if I could ask . . ."

The man kept walking, still looking off at some point in the distance.

He should've expected that reaction. He didn't go to the same meetings Rich did, so why should he be acknowledged? And Nick's clothes—khaki pants, JC Penny plaid shirt—probably didn't help either. Rich's shiny leather loafers squeaked as he continued down the hall. Must be new, Nick thought. *I have clothes like that too*, he wanted to call down the hall . . . *even the suspenders*. His mother had bought him oxford shirts and pleated slacks for Christmas, but still, he couldn't bring himself to wear them. It felt too much like surrender.

He took the stairs two steps at a time, stomping down hard, but the rubber soles of his Docksiders gave off only weak, muffled slaps against the padded carpeting. Every conference room on the second floor was full. Employees turned bored gazes to the windows as he passed. He didn't recognize anyone. Finally, he stopped in an empty hallway near the pantry, by the fire exit, hands on hips, face hot.

Over the fire door was a red illuminated EXIT sign. He pictured himself crossing the lot, an easy swing to his stride, and speeding away. Driving with the windows down, tapes blaring, he'd take some road never taken before. Just thinking about it filled his body with a pleasant lightness.

Two managers from Customer Service, a man and a woman, were walking his way, carrying coffee cups big as goblets. He didn't know their names. He wished he had papers or a folder, something to carry, to look at. Nobody stood around with only a Bic ballpoint pen in his hand.

The man was short and bowlegged. His round belly seemed to start at his groin and extend halfway up his chest. He grinned at Nick. "Does the bus stop here?"

"I wish it would," Nick muttered.

The woman wore a stiff gray suit. She was thin, all jagged angles, with a wrinkled face and tight curly silver hair. "I've been waiting fifteen years. Haven't seen it yet!" she said with a sharp laugh.

They disappeared around the corner. Nick paced the hallway, gripping the pen like a knife. He'd been in this job for more than a year and had never done anything wrong. Never even been late. Not out of duty or responsibility, though everybody seemed to mistake it for that, but because it was the best way to stay unnoticed. Show up on time, process the right amount of invoices, and he could be as anonymous as the computer monitors on all the desks. Indifference was comforting. When he was nobody, nothing could touch him.

He lingered by the fire exit. The longer he took to find this class or whatever, the more of a big deal Deborah would make out of it. He'd be summoned to her office and possibly get a write-up. He wasn't sure what those were, exactly, but she threatened the clerks with them all the time. Maybe he should just leave. This was too stupid to get worked up about. He could leave and go try doing something new. Weren't there people who did that? What kind of jobs did Dag Nasty have before they'd started the band? Did they make enough money to live on now? He sighed, trying to settle his thoughts. The problem was, he had no specific talent for anything. He couldn't imagine his escape going any further than zipping a few miles down Route 518 blasting 7 Seconds with the windows down.

The sticker on the fire door read ALARM WILL SOUND WHEN DOOR IS OPENED.

He turned away and continued down a hallway lined with motivational prints. The huge photographic posters had captions like *Excellence. Freedom. Vision.* A basketball player making a layup in a crowd of defenders. An eagle soaring over a lake. A mountain climber on a snowy peak, arms raised in victory. *Perseverance: It's the only way to achieve your wildest dreams.*

Nick stared at the picture of the mountain climber. What was the guy cheering about? All alone on the top of a freezing cold mountain.

He climbed the steps, right knee aching whenever he put weight on it. He'd caught the heel of a boot there at the end of the show. He shook his head. It felt now like last night had never happened. He opened the stairwell door to the third floor, recalling the Circle Jerks loading their equipment in the rain, a towel held over their heads. They were from California. They'd made jokes about hippies and Haight Ashbury. Probably drove that old van across the whole country just to go out and perform. They could do all that yet he couldn't even say *You know what? I don't need this job or any of this other useless crap.*

The third floor was ringed by more conference rooms, where men in ties sat around polished tables. In the lobby, two large red-faced guys in suits leaned on a counter behind which sat a young receptionist. The men, who were chatting and laughing over her head, turned to look at Nick. "You the guy from Sales?" one asked.

"No."

He looked Nick up and down. "Didn't think so!" he said, then laughed.

The other man slapped his companion on the back and grinned. "*This* guy. He's nothing but trouble."

"Hey, it couldn't hurt to ask, right?"

The receptionist, young, with long brown hair pulled back in a ponytail, ignored them all and continued typing, her smooth face blank. Nick kept walking. What the hell were they laughing about? That wasn't even funny. He heard that kind of empty laughter in the office a lot, usually accompanied by those aggressive smiles that were really only the quick baring of teeth. No happiness behind it at all.

He rounded a corner and saw a blue glow spilling from the open door of a conference room. Inside, people were seated in rows, silhouetted against the computer monitors in front of them. A man spoke at the front, standing beside a projection screen. Nick recognized Sharon and Tina, two of the other accounting clerks, by the flower-bouquet shape of their teased-out hairdos against the light of the monitors. He slipped into the dark room and found a seat between the two young women. It was the same hierarchy wherever they went. Meeting, class, or luncheon. Senior staff in front. Accountants in the middle. Clerks in the back.

Sharon narrowed her eyes at him and hissed, "Did Deborah see you?" When he nodded, she widened them as if terrified about his fate.

Nick didn't want to hear it. He tapped Tina's shoulder and whispered, "What's this thing about?"

She blinked and shrugged. "I went to sleep the minute he turned off the lights. Who the hell has a class at seven-thirty in the morning?"

"Does anyone have any questions at this point?" the man at the front said. "I mean, anyone beside the guy who just walked in."

Heads turned in Nick's direction. Chuckles rippled through the room. He curled his lips in a smile to show what a good sport he was.

"Well, OK then," the presenter said. "Moving on."

The class continued for another hour. It seemed they were going to be using a new computer program. Nick didn't get any of it, but he sat and randomly clicked on the keyboard along with everyone else. At last, the presenter said, "Thank you, everybody, for coming." He flicked on the lights and the class rose and shuffled to the door. Everyone carried instruction books. Tina had already scribbled doodles all over the cover of hers: curlicues and flowers, black circles inside all the O's in *OmniFlow Operations Guide*.

She patted Nick lightly on the back. "You are *so* screwed."

One of the senior guys, who usually never spoke to him, laughed as he passed. "You get all that, Nick?"

More jokes followed as people filed past. He knew this verbal hazing would last for the next few days. The slightest transgression or mishap could be turned into great entertainment in his department. The college intern, last fall, had stumbled and spilled an entire bowl of soup across her white blouse in the cafeteria. One of the senior accountants had come running back to the department to tell everybody about it. "Just like a wet t-shirt contest," he kept saying.

Nick crossed his arms and bowed his head, avoiding his reflection in the conference room windows. He pictured the guy in that poster, arms raised in solitary victory. Now it made sense. *He wasn't on that mountaintop to achieve his wildest dreams*, Nick thought. *He was just trying to get away from all of you.*

"I don't know what happened this morning," Deborah said. "And I don't want to know."

They were in her office. She sat behind the desk, a leather-bound appointment book open in front of her. She'd waited until after lunch to call him in. Nick tried to lean back in the metal-framed chair but his back was too sore from last night. He propped his elbows on the narrow arms and tried not to slouch. His mouth was dry, but why should he be nervous? Maybe it was time to stop being so obedient. No, not *maybe*. It was past time.

Deborah pushed back her sleeves. She always wore lots of things on her wrists. A silver Rolex watch. Clunky brightly-colored plastic bracelets or a bunch of slender gold chains. She was constantly touching and adjusting them. "We're rolling out this new program next Monday and you missed the training. You're going to have no idea what to do."

She paused to give him time to consider the grave consequences of this mistake. He opened his mouth to speak, but she continued. "I was relying on you to learn this because, well, between you and me, you know Sharon and Tina can't do it. Those two probably slept through the entire class." She picked up a pen and wrote a quick note in her appointment book. "I'll talk to one of the senior guys and see if they can find the time to show it to you again. But they're swamped so don't waste too much of their time."

"It's OK. We don't need to bother."

She put down her pen. "No. You need to learn this. You can't do your job without it."

Nick stared. He usually couldn't look anybody in the eye for long, but with Deborah he could. She gazed back the way she looked at everybody: as an annoyance to be dealt with, like a sheet of paper jammed in the printer or a broken pencil. Nick usually found that reassuring, but today he wanted to be heard. There were things he wanted to say, about this job, this whole place. But already, facing her annoyed glare, the words were fading away.

"Don't think you can just wing it, Nick. You've got the best turnaround time in the department, but that'll go in the toilet if you don't know how this new software works."

Her office was in the center of the building, so there were no windows. Above lay three floors of computers and typewriters and file cabinets and desks. People pacing carpeted hallways, opening and closing metal drawers, rolling on swivel chairs, gathering around conference tables, leaning into speakerphones, standing in doorways, sipping coffee from ceramic mugs they'd brought in from home. Talking about the weather, the traffic, last night's TV shows. Saying whatever they were supposed to say. Doing what they were supposed to do.

Whatever he'd been going to say evaporated. "I thought I could . . ." He coughed. His voice was hoarse. "I thought I could probably figure it out by myself."

She stared. "You're joking. The class took more than three hours and you're going to teach yourself."

He shrugged. "That way I wouldn't have to bother anybody."

"Well. At least that shows initiative. But there's no way you can figure this out by yourself." She opened a folder. "You know, Nick, I have to be honest. I'm not sure what you want from this job. Your numbers are great. Ninety percent within net 30. The best 2/10 record in the department."

He knew all this meant something in the bigger machinery of the corporation, but to him it was just a game to see how quickly he could memorize account numbers and apply them to stacks of invoices.

She closed the folder and set it on top of a neat pile of other folders. "And Data Entry tells me they hardly ever need to do any adjusting on your accounts. Your coding is all very clean."

He never saw the people in Data Entry. They knew him only by the cards he left in their bins at noon and 4:00 every day, the ones with his tiny square numbers on them and the cramped *Nick LaBlanche* scrawled at the bottom. He wished he could communicate with everyone that way: just hand them a card with the pertinent information and then go back to his cubicle.

Deborah was still talking, so Nick nodded intently. "But that's it. You show up, do your job, and leave. You don't get involved in anything. Don't interact with anybody. You just go along with everything."

He frowned. "And . . . that's bad?"

"Well, it's not going to get you anywhere."

"Where is it I'm supposed to be going?" he asked, but she spoke right over him.

"I'm serious, Nick. You have to ask yourself: where do I want to be five years from now? No offense, but you sit in your cubicle and do your little invoices and that's great, don't misunderstand, but you don't really show any *motivation*. I mean, your output is fantastic. But where's the drive?"

Whenever she moved her hands—which was often—her gold bracelet shook. Her Rolex winked at him in the overhead lights.

"You can't tell, sitting down here on the bottom floor in your own little world. But the way things are out there, you either go after what you want or you're going to get run over. Things are changing, with this buyout coming up. You need to make yourself visible. Tina and Sharon don't understand this, but I think you do."

He mumbled something he'd heard on a radio commercial, something about banking on the future. He'd intended to say it forcefully but the words faltered coming out of his mouth.

Deborah propped her elbows on the edge of her desk. "You need to think of ways to get yourself noticed. Ways to stand out. Do something before you get stuck in a real rut. Which reminds me—I meant to ask you something."

She glanced down at the appointment book. "I was looking at your file. How come you never went on to college?"

He shifted in his seat. "I took some classes at the community college for a semester, right after high school." After the first week he'd begun skipping classes to spend entire days at the library randomly picking out books. For some reason he'd kept returning to the Philosophy section: lots of Sartre and Nietzsche. By the time midterms came around he'd forgotten the room numbers of his classes. "But I didn't really have enough money to continue," he added, then shrugged and grimaced in what he hoped was a suitable expression of regret.

"See?" She nodded. "There's an opportunity right there. The company will pay for your classes. You can take one or two at night. Of course, they'd have to be business classes. You could probably ace accounting right off the bat."

In high school, accounting had been the only thing he was good at. There was something about the order and balance of it he'd liked. It completely ignored reality.

"Look, I'm not trying to put you on the spot. But you have to ask yourself: what do I want from this job? How can it get me to where I want to be?"

"Sure. Like a will to power kind of thing."

"I don't know what that means." Deborah shook her head. "Have you read *In Search of Excellence* by Tom Peters?"

"I don't think I've heard of that one."

"You should. He asks those kinds of questions. Things you should be asking yourself."

He nodded. "*In Search of Excellence*," he repeated. "OK, sure. Thanks."

He continued nodding while she watched him. Finally, he stopped and just stared at the top of her desk. Next to her appointment book three pens were lined up, red, black and blue, all pointing in the same direction.

"Well?"

He looked up. "Well . . . what?"

She crossed her arms and leaned forward. The flat shoulder pads of her suit extended too far past her shoulders. She looked like a jet about to take off. "Where do you want to be? What do you want from this job?"

He let a long "uhhhh . . ." and cleared his throat. Nobody had ever asked him what he wanted before, about anything.

She raised one eyebrow. His face tightened like a mask, until he couldn't tell if he was smiling or wincing. He stared down at his feet and rubbed his chin in a pantomime of contemplation. "I . . . I don't really think about . . ."

The carpeting in Deborah's office was the standard gray industrial kind, just like in the therapist's office he used to go to as a teenager. That office had been in a suite of doctors' offices on a tree-lined street in Princeton. His mother would wait in the car and do crossword puzzles while inside Nick and the therapist played backgammon. Nick hardly spoke, and eventually the therapist stopped asking any questions, but he could always feel the man watching his face as he contemplated his next move.

"Take your time with it," Deborah said finally, turning away, paging through her appointment book. "Get back to me later."

In the tiny pantry right outside their department, Sharon and Tina stood by the coffee machine, leaning into each other. Nick could tell by the harsh hiss of their whispers that they were talking about Deborah again.

"She can't make us come in early," Sharon said. "We're not all yuppie scum-queens like her."

"I know." Tina nodded. "She's just using us to make herself look good, as if she's some real boss."

Sharon yawned, manicured fingers cupping her mouth. "God, I still can't wake up." She looked over at Nick, behind them. "I should've blown it off like you."

"I didn't do it on purpose," he said.

They turned to face him, coffee mugs in hand. They both wore long, tight skirts and shimmering silk blouses. "How bad did she chew you out?" Tina raised an eyebrow.

"Not too much."

"Figures." She rolled her eyes at Sharon. "If it'd had been one of us our ass would be out the door."

Sharon yawned again. "Or at least get a write-up."

They both nodded at each other as if he wasn't there.

"It wasn't like she was happy about it." Nick shuffled towards the coffee maker, trying to mimic their lazy resignation, the off-handed fatalism, but he could never do it without feeling awkward.

"I need some sleep," Sharon said. "I'm going out tonight."

"Where to?"

"Oh, we're going to bounce around. It's lady's night at the Fizz, then there's the Buttondown Café. Dollar shots. Maybe check out the guidos at the Granada. It's going to be a major bar hop."

"Cool."

"You're totally missing out, Nick," Sharon said.

"What am I missing, exactly?"

"He doesn't go anywhere," Tina said. "Even if he was old enough."

"Ever go to the 321 Club? I was—" Nick stopped himself. "I heard it was kind of cool."

Sharon winced. "That's in Trenton, right?"

"I think I was there once," Tina said. "They have, like, super-cheap drinks."

"I know that place," Sharon said. "I heard some girl got beat up with a pool cue there."

"*You* go to bars?" Tina asked Nick.

He attempted a nonchalant shrug. "Sometimes."

She sipped her coffee, holding the mug with two hands. "They play this music there that makes you want to beat your head against a wall. And holy shit, it's a freakshow."

"Some of that music's pretty good, actually," Nick said, keeping his gaze on his coffee mug.

"No cool guys though, huh?" Sharon asked, speaking over him.

"Nope. And the place is a shithole." Tina shuddered. "That freaking parking lot. I broke the heel off my favorite shoes trying to walk out of there."

"Which ones?" Sharon frowned. "The stilettos?"

"No. The velvet pumps with the little black bows in the front."

"Oh," Sharon said ruefully. "I never saw them."

"I like some of that music," Nick added.

Deborah appeared in the doorway, no coffee cup in hand. *"What are you guys doing?"*

"Just getting coffee," Nick said.

"Taking my break," Sharon said.

"Yep." Tina nodded. "Coffee break."

They raised their mugs.

"All three of you? Who's watching the phones?"

They strolled back to their cubicles. Once they were a safe distance away, Sharon said under her breath, "Who *calls* us? Nobody even knows we're down here."

"Seriously," Nick said. He had matched his pace to their slow, grudging stride.

Sharon rolled her eyes. "She wasn't even looking at you, Nick."

By the end of the day he'd coded and dropped off one hundred and seventeen invoices. It was easier than thinking. He sat in his cubicle and waited for the five o'clock rush of people to leave. He stared at the fabric of the wall: a weave of crisscrossing yarns of pale blue, white, royal blue, gray, silver, a little bit of black. From a distance, the walls all looked light gray. No one could tell they were made up of different colors unless they got really close. There must be some meaning to draw from this, but his mind felt like a bell that had been rung too many times.

At ten after five, he went to Tina's cubicle, took the instruction book off her desk and headed upstairs to the conference room on the third floor. The program from that morning was still on the screens. He took a seat in the corner, away from the door, opened the book and went to work. In the hallway outside people said their good nights. Within half an hour he'd finished every lesson. It was easy. No big deal. He rose, scowling, took the book back to Tina's desk and left. He recalled how he had raced up the stairs that morning. How nervous, how panicked and thoughtless, he'd been in Deborah's office. And for what? All he wanted to do now was put his fist through his face.

Heading out the front, he ended up alongside a man in a suit carrying a gym bag over one shoulder. It was early spring but the guy already had a deep tan. He glanced at Nick's face. "Damn! Rough day, huh?"

Nick shrugged. "Yeah. I guess."

They ended up walking together across the parking lot. Their cars were parked next to each other.

"You know what they say." The man grinned. "'What doesn't kill you makes you stronger.'"

Nietzsche. Everybody got that quote wrong. "That's supposed to be irony, I think," Nick said. "I think Nietzsche meant it ironically. He was talking about his drill sergeant and, uh . . ."

His voice trailed off. He wasn't sure if the name was pronounced *Nee-chee* or *Nee-cha*. He'd never had to say it out loud before.

The man looked Nick up and down as if just noticing he was actually there. "Cool," he said, with convincing sincerity. "That's good to know."

Nick thought, *This guy must be a very good salesman.*

When he started his car a quick roar of guitars blasted out of the speakers. Immediately, he saw the crowd from last night, writhing like a massive snake beneath the stage lights. Recalled the way the singer from Dag Nasty had dived into the pit. Head first. No hesitation. Why did he even think he could ever be part of that? He popped out the tape and threw it in the back seat.

The traffic was a continuous stream down Route 206, but he pulled blindly out into it. The truck he cut in front of honked but he didn't even look back. Once he'd ejected the tape the top 40 station came on. He left it: something mindless to get him home. He sat through three commercials and then some synthesized love song started. *Hold me now, in your loving arms.* The synthesizers and muffled drums sounded like the hushed whirring of the computer on his desk at work. He scowled and pressed a button for another preset station and caught the guitar solo at the end of *Comfortably Numb*.

"*Pink Floyd, from* The Wall *album*," the sleepy-voiced DJ said.

Nick rolled his eyes: as if anybody had to be reminded. This station only played Pink Floyd and Led Zeppelin, and every once in a while that song about dust in the wind.

"*On the other side of this, we'll have Led Zep and some Kansas . . .*"

He listened to the opening of "Stairway to Heaven." In junior high a kid in the back of the school bus had played that every morning on his boom box. The whole bus would go quiet as if it were morning prayers. He recalled the sickening smell of diesel fumes and the stiff green plastic seats, then tuned to the other rock station. Some band was rocking like a hurricane, guitar chords dropping like dinosaur steps.

Cars stopped in a clump at the busy traffic light to turn for Route 518, the long narrow road that led back to Hopewell. He considered shutting off the radio, but didn't want to sit in this traffic listening to the engine idling, inching forward and stopping, body indistinguishable from his car, just another machine to pump the brake and grip the steering wheel.

Once on 518 he fell into the slow, unbroken column of vehicles and tuned to TSR, Trenton State College's station. Silence. Maybe they were off the air.

The line stretched far ahead. The sun slowly sank behind the trees. Shadows deepened and porch lights came on in the square, well-tended houses along the roadside. He was so sleepy from the monotony of work he felt like he was sinking into the driver's seat, melting into the synthetic upholstery. In the rear-view mirror he glimpsed the blank-eyed face of the man in the car behind him. In all the cars behind that one the same silhouette was repeated, a lone driver in each car, hands on the steering wheel, staring straight ahead.

Just then, from the speakers came the crackle of a needle in the vinyl groove of a record. A whine of feedback. Bass and the drums kicked in, rumbling and rattling like someone tumbling down a flight of metal steps. Jagged guitar chords repeated themselves in an anxious rhythm. He stared at the speaker grille. A string of red brake lights extended for a mile ahead in the deepening dusk. He turned up the volume.

A ragged voice sang, *"But I woke up this morning, with a piece of past caught in my throat."*

He cranked the volume knob again, not sure what he was hearing. The man's voice was desperate and frayed. The tiny speakers in Nick's Chevette buzzed like hornets. The music filled the car and beat around his ears like fists. He pulled down on the thick knot of his knit tie, bobbing his head and bouncing in his seat. The mask he'd been maintaining for the last eight hours fractured and dropped away.

"And then I choked."

The song churned, building, pushing itself faster, about to fall apart at any second.

3

VICTORIA

Nick was standing in the crowd at the front of the stage at the 321 Club, waiting for the Descendants to come on, when Victoria came up and took his hand. He hadn't seen her since that first time at the show last week, but for some reason wasn't startled. He didn't flinch.

She wove her fingers through his, pale eyes fixed on his face. "You never told me your name."

Her leather biker jacket was unzipped and pulled back off her shoulders. She wore what looked like a long black slip underneath. The silver choke chain around her neck had a tiny padlock just below her throat linking the two rings at the ends. Hardcore blasted over the PA system, so he had to lean in close, his mouth to her ear, to say his name. Her perfume smelled like crushed roses.

"Who are you here with?" she asked. Her breath was warm against his neck.

"No one."

She leaned back to look at him, their faces inches apart. The PA went silent. The crowd cheered and whooped as four musicians stepped onto the stage, picked up guitars and adjusted the microphone stands. She said something, her thin red lips shaping words.

"I can't hear you," Nick said.

She pressed her mouth to his. The drummer counted off and guitars roared out of the speakers at the side of the stage. Victoria parted her lips and their tongues touched. She held his hand tightly. Nick wrapped an arm around her waist. The singer howled, *"Don't wanna spend the rest of my days in yesterday's daydreams."* The thudding bass and stomping boots made the floor beneath them shudder. She laid a palm on the side of his face and held the kiss, her tongue searching his mouth. Someone bumped his back and their teeth knocked together. She laughed, her forehead pressed to his.

She pulled him by the hand through the crowd, away from the stage. Around them people leaped and pumped fists in the air. A boy with a towering mohawk wouldn't get out of her way. She drove her free elbow into his chest and plowed forward, finally finding an empty spot between the pit and the bar. A few people, older, dressed simply in jeans and t-shirts or flannel shirts, leaned against the bar, turned so they could watch the band.

"Wow," he said. "You knocked that guy on his ass."

She glanced back like she'd already forgotten about it. "He was an asshole."

She wrapped her arms around his neck and held him tightly, breasts pressing against his chest. He hugged her back and inhaled the smells of leather and perfume and cigarettes. She was as tall as he was, her shoulders almost as broad. Their bodies seemed to shadow each other.

"Look," she said, turning her head. Her hair had been cut so closely along the side of her head that there were tiny pink scratches beneath the pale blonde fuzz. "Look at the pit."

In front of the stage a tight wall of people had formed a circle. Within it, upraised arms flailed. The singer stood at the edge of the stage, bent over and screaming. A shirtless boy was up on someone's shoulders, snapping punches in the air. Another, crowned with an orange mohawk, climbed up someone's back. The two charged at each other through the mass. They collided in a tumble of limbs and then dropped into the crowd. Another skinhead boy was hoisted up onto someone's shoulders. The bouncers at the side of the stage waved at him to get down.

She smiled. "Chicken fights."

"It looks like they're jousting."

"I love the pit." She bit her lower lip. Nick watched her face, unable to decide if she was pretty or not. She brought his hand to her lips and held the index finger between her teeth. Her tongue circled slowly and warmly around his fingertip.

"I don't know where to go," he said.

"Let's see."

She led him back behind the bar to the spot where he'd first seen her last week. Her friends were there, again sitting on the footrest: the two girls who'd been following him around and one other he'd never seen before.

"What are you guys doing here?" Victoria said. "The Descendants are on."

The new girl was short and chubby. Her hair looked like a messy haystack of greens and oranges and blues.

"This is Rat." Victoria pointed at her. "Rat, this is Nick."

Nick said "Hi" and pulled his army jacket around him to cover his erection. The girl waved and grinned then shyly ducked her head.

"This is Crow."

The thin, dark-haired girl exhaled a plume of smoke and blinked at him.

"And this is Bird."

The little blonde girl screwed up her face in an imitation of a tough guy—lips in a sneer, eyes squinting, cigarette clenched between her teeth. "Right on, Nick," she said, shooting him a thumbs-up sign.

"It's a regular menagerie," he said.

The girl named Crow turned to the blonde girl. "Did he just say 'ménage a trois'?"

Bird shook her head. "Optimistic fella, isn't he?"

Victoria had not let go his hand. "Why aren't you guys checking out the band?"

"Too much static," Bird said. "These skinheads came up from Philadelphia. Said they weren't gonna take any crap from Jersey skins."

"And they're all ugly as shit too!" Crow threw up her hands. "No cute guys anywhere." To Nick, she said, "Except for you, of course."

"Yeah," Bird said. "You're so *pret-ty*."

The girl named Rat giggled and kneaded the bottom of her long white t-shirt. Just like last time, Nick couldn't tell if he was being mocked or not. He wanted to say something, but felt like an old car trying to pull onto a busy highway.

"We're going outside," Victoria said.

Bird shrugged. Every gesture of hers seemed disapproving. "Stay out of the infield."

As they headed for the door, he asked, "What did she mean?"

"Who knows," she said. "Bird doesn't like to make sense. It's how she entertains herself."

They got their hands stamped at the door, then crossed the parking lot, moving away from the bright flood light that hung over the entrance. Skinheads in flight jackets stood in a circle. One threw a bottle straight up in the air. They all watched it as it shattered on the pavement.

"You flinched!" one said.

"Fuck! I got glass on me."

They turned and stared at Nick, then at Victoria, and seemed to decide something without saying a word. They turned their backs again and one skinhead threw another bottle in the air.

At the end of the lot, behind a chain-link fence, was a baseball field overgrown with tall weeds. They found a hole in the rusty wire, crouched through, and then climbed onto the metal bleachers. She sat with her legs across his lap. They kissed again and again, grabbing at each other's clothes, Victoria pulling up his t-shirt to run her fingernails down his belly, Nick slipping her leather jacket off and sliding the straps of her slip down, palms lightly touching her breasts, Victoria lying back on the bleachers, jacket beneath her, fingers unbuttoning the top of his jeans, sliding the zipper down, Nick, hands trembling, fumbling at the waistband of her underwear, Victoria sliding them down the curve of her hips and over the narrow heels of her tall black boots.

"So glad I didn't wear my Doc Martens tonight or this would be difficult."

Over the cursing and laughing of the skinheads and the occasional shatter of glass they could hear the band, bass and drums muffled and thumping like a giant heart behind the concrete walls of the club. The white glare of the floodlight blinded him. She was a pale silhouette beneath him, fingers clutching his shoulders, pulling him down. The glare was so bright it lit up the inside of his skull. He turned his face the other way and saw the long shadows of tall weeds swaying across the baseball field. She held on as if she was falling, breath gasping quick and warm in his ear. She kissed his face, his mouth, his chin, lips tracing down his throat, and then sank her teeth into his neck and held fast. A cold shiver ran down his body and he let out a long sigh. She kissed him softly on the side of his face.

He propped himself up on his elbows. "I'm sorry," he said. "That was so quick."

Her hands felt along his throat and over his face. She touched his mouth, pressed his lips closed. "It's OK. I did too, a little."

He looked around. "Why is it so quiet?"

The side doors of the club hung open. No music from inside, only yelling.

"Something must've happened," she said.

People streamed out of the club and scattered across the parking lot. He quickly zipped his pants. After some fumbling around, he found her underwear and handed them to her. She pulled him closer and he lifted his arms to hug her.

"No," she said, stopping him. "Stand right there so you can block the light." She sat down on the bottom row of bleachers and bent to work her underwear up over her boots. "Don't watch. I look like a ho doing this."

They crouched through the hole in the fence and, holding hands, wound their way back through the crowded lot. Bouncers stood by the open doors of the club, waving big flashlights.

Some girl was hollering "Vic-*ky*!" over and over again. The little blond girl, Bird. "Hey!" she said to them. "We gotta book."

"What happened?" Victoria asked.

"This kid got pulverized by the Crew. There was blood, like, all over the floor. The band stopped playing and said they wouldn't come back."

"The Crew?" Nick said.

"The local skinhead cub scout troop." Bird had not looked at Nick until then. "They think this is their club," she said.

Victoria shrugged. "They're not so bad most of the time."

"As rabid pit bulls go, yeah, they're swell. There's Crow and those guys. Let's go before the cops show up and we all get stuck here."

A rust-spotted Oldsmobile pulled up. Nick couldn't count how many were in the car, it was so full. Hands and arms dangled out the windows.

"Give me a pen," Victoria said.

Bird flipped open the chest pocket of her denim jacket and pulled out a bundle of pens and pencils bound with a rubber band. Victoria yanked out a Sharpie, took Nick's hand and wrote a phone number on his palm.

"Let's go, Vic." Bird opened the car door for her. "I get the front."

"Whose lap am I going to sit on?" Victoria climbed awkwardly over the people packed in the back seat. Bird held the car door, watching Nick the whole time, chin raised, her round girlish face a blank. Not knowing what else to do, he waved. Bird did nothing, just stared with the bold, clear-eyed gaze of a child.

He stood with his hands at his sides as if for inspection. "What?" he said finally.

"Have fun slumming?"

"What are you talking about?"

The corner of her mouth lifted in a wry grin. "Weird place to take a vacation, dude."

Now he knew what she meant. He'd experienced it that first night among the crowd at the bar, the way some people had glared like he was a tourist. And tonight, as he came through the door, someone had muttered *poser* in his direction.

Nick looked down at Bird—she was a full foot shorter than him—and tried to match her confident gaze. "I want to be here."

She shrugged. "If you say so."

"I don't have any place else to go."

Which was true, but out loud it sounded pathetic.

She finally stopped staring and nodded, eyes downcast, then walked around to the front passenger seat. Just before she got in, she held up a hand and waved at him with one finger. The car pulled forward, easing into the line leaving the lot.

All around him, car stereos blasted a dozen different hardcore songs, the bellowing voices and crashing guitars coming together into one long continuous roar.

4

CLICK

At work the next morning, he stared at the fabric of the cubicle wall. Pale blue, white, royal blue, gray, silver and a few threads of black. He tried to replay what had happened the night before, but the more he thought about it, the more the feelings evaporated. He could not even summon a clear memory of Victoria's face.

Tina dropped a stack of invoices in his inbox. "I got these by mistake."

He flipped through. Tina had mixed in some of her own vendors' invoices. "These are yours, aren't they?"

"Technically, yeah." She shrugged. "But you're fast. You've done them before."

"I have plenty right here. I'm going to fall behind."

"Not you, Nick. You're the super accounts payable guy."

"Not if I keep doing other people's work," he mumbled, then regretted it. He didn't want to make the newfound animosity between him and Tina and Sharon any worse. They were still insulted he wasn't in trouble for missing that class, while they were always scolded by Deborah for the slightest mistake. They'd stopped speaking, which bothered him more than he'd thought it would. He knew little about Tina and Sharon, but had always thought of them as comrades-in-arms, fellow sufferers of the office tedium, even though they'd fall over laughing if he ever said words like that out loud.

As Tina turned to go, she glanced at his neck and froze. "Whoa, check you out. Did you get the name of that vampire?"

"I met this girl . . ."

"No shit. Really? I wouldn't have known if you didn't tell me."

She laughed as she walked away. "Way to go, Nick," she called over the cubicle wall. "You're not half the geek I thought you were."

Why had he bothered saying anything? He never talked to the people at work about his personal life. He touched the tender spot on his neck, trying to convince himself it had really happened.

He called Victoria that night after dinner.

An older man with a deep voice answered. He guessed it was her father. "She's at a friend's house studying." He sounded like he was biting off the ends of the words. "What's this about?"

"I'm a—a friend of hers."

"From school?"

"No. The 321 Club."

The man let out a disgruntled sigh. "Great."

Nick left his number and got off as quickly and courteously as he could. He picked through his albums and decided on Public Image Limited. Something pounding and repetitive to drive all thoughts out of his head. Who knew if she'd call back? Maybe it had been just a one-time thing. He paced around his room, put out a shirt and slacks and tie for the next day, paced some more. The last time he'd talked to a girl on the phone was his junior year of high school: a brief phase of trying to be social which had actually gotten him a date. A plain-faced girl who wore clogs and a lot of heavy, itchy sweaters. They'd dated for four months. Before calling her, he would prepare a mental list of things to talk about. Eventually, the list ran out. By their senior year they were passing each other in the halls like strangers.

He was about to put on another album when the phone rang.

"Hold on," Victoria said when he picked up. A man and woman were yelling in the background. "I have to switch phones."

"You all right?" he asked when she got back on.

"Yeah. I'm fine. At home."

"Your dad said you were out studying."

"He always says that. I was at Al-Anon. I go there every Monday and Wednesday. My parents don't want anybody to know." Her voice was soft and hushed like a whisper. "Did you get home OK last night?"

"Yeah. No problems."

The phone clicked and then there were beeps as a number was dialed. "I'm on the phone," Victoria said.

"Hello?" a woman said.

"*Mom*, I'm on the phone."

"Jesus Christ, Vicky. I'm trying to make a call."

"But *I'm* on the phone right now."

A sigh and the receiver was slammed down.

Victoria sighed. "Sometimes I miss the center. Nobody bothered me there."

"The center?"

"They put me in a psychiatric facility for two weeks. It wasn't so bad, except I couldn't listen to any of my music. Did you ever have to go to one?"

"Once. When I was, I guess 14. But I didn't stay."

"My first time there, I met this boy in the lobby while I was waiting for the psychologist. He saw the bandages on my wrists and said, 'That was stupid.'"

The phone line clicked again.

"I thought how sweet this stranger is saying it's stupid to throw my life away. And then he goes, 'Don't you know you're supposed to cut lengthwise along the wrist, not across it?'"

"Victoria! Christ, who wants to hear that stuff?"

"Dad. I'm having a conversation."

"Your mother needs the phone. Stop making her life difficult."

"I need a minute."

The phone clicked off and she sighed. "Guess I better go."

"OK."

"Who's your favorite hardcore band?"

"7 Seconds, I guess. They're hardcore, right?"

"Of course. I have *Walk Together, Rock Together*. I'm going to lock myself in my room and play it over and over again."

"I have that one. I'll play it the same time you do."

She giggled. "We're like so twelve years old."

"It's funny."

"Give me five minutes, then put it on."

He dropped the album onto the turntable, sat on the floor beside the record player, and waited. He wondered if she'd gone to the same center his father tried to take him to. Five years ago, but he still remembered the antiseptic pine-and-vinegar smell, the fluorescent lights reflecting off freshly-mopped linoleum. The waiting area had been full of other boys, all bored and pale and tired. Only one other had a parent with him. Everyone kept their heads down and shifted in their seats. Nick and his father stood and waited for twenty minutes. There was no place to sit. His father kept shuffling his feet and jingling the change in his pocket, but Nick felt oddly at home. Maybe only because here you didn't have to pretend you were OK.

"Forget about this," his father had said finally and headed for the door, scowling, face red. Nick had hesitated in the waiting area, not sure if he was supposed to follow or not. The other boys watched him. When his father held the door open and motioned him over, he was surprised: it seemed like a very fatherly thing to do.

Now he lowered the needle onto the record. The first song began in a quick blur of guitars, the drums fast as a blender. *"You wanna be the way I am but you could never understand."* The singer's voice was earnest and fierce. He sang so fast the lyrics were a jumble of syllables run together, as if there was only so much time to say what he had to say before people stopped listening.

Nick drew his knees up to his chest, bowed his head and shut his eyes. He let the music course through him. He pictured the smoke-filled club, the crowded pit, the waves of people crashing like surf against the stage. He pictured Victoria in her room imagining these same things.

Early the next morning, Deborah appeared in his cubicle. He looked up, startled, then snatched up a pen. He'd been sitting, hands on his desk, staring at invoices, thinking about nothing.

"Did you finish your job description?"

His mouth dropped open. "Uh . . ."

"I'm going up to Corporate. I need all the job descriptions. I don't have yours yet."

"I'm still working on it." He shuffled the invoices in front of him.

"How much do you have done?"

"Not much."

"Is that it?" She pointed at the only piece of paper on his desk that wasn't an invoice or a purchase order.

"I need to, I need to start over."

She sighed. "Just give it to me."

He shook his head, then gave up. He handed over the paper without looking at her. All he'd filled out was his name, job title, and the year he'd started. Under Job Role, he'd scribbled *Terminal Preppie*. The title of a Dead Kennedys song.

"God, Nick." Her face showed no anger or disappointment or anything. "Do I have to do this myself?" She turned on one heel and stalked back to her office.

He followed. "You don't have to do it at all," he said. "I don't understand the point of this. Everybody here knows what we do."

She sat down behind her desk and tugged the cuffs of her blazer down. "No. The people up there—" She pointed an index finger at the ceiling. "—have no idea who you are or what you do. This is your chance to sell yourself." She read the paper over again, shaking her head. "I don't know what's going on with you. I can't take this up there." She folded the paper in half and dropped it in the wastebasket. "Did you ever sign up for those college classes?"

"Not yet."

"Do it, and give me a copy of your registration right away."

He adjusted the knot of his tie. For some reason he couldn't keep his hands still. He'd never spoken up at work before. So he didn't know how to act when he said, "I don't know if I want to take any classes."

His boss's eyes widened. "Didn't we talk about this?"

"I don't understand why I need to do any of this stuff."

"Because it's your future. We talked about it."

He put his hands in his pockets, then took them out. Went to fix his tie again, but stopped himself. She looked startled, or maybe confused. She re-arranged the three pens on her desk, lining them up in a different order but still so they all pointed in the same direction.

Though he'd never acted like this at work, something pushed him on. "I don't understand why we have to go through this pretense. I mean, why *I* have to. You said I'm doing a good job."

She peered at her Rolex. "I have to be in Corporate in two minutes. What's your point? Is this about those two?" She cocked her head toward Sharon's and Tina's cubicles. "Did they say something to you?"

"I can think for myself."

"Because, believe me," she continued as if he hadn't said a word, "Those girls are the last people you want career advice from."

"I don't understand why we have to make up all this stuff about 'career goals.' I do a good job. I show up. I do all my work. Then go home."

"Right."

"Isn't that enough?"

"No, it isn't. They want to know your goals."

"What if those *are* my goals? Show up, do a good job, go home?"

She rolled her eyes and checked her watch again. "Tell me again: what's the point of this conversation?"

"I just don't understand why you're helping me all the time. You don't even know me. Maybe I'm not the super accounts payable guy you think I am. Why are you making these assumptions?"

She said nothing, but something clicked behind her dark impassive eyes. She paged through the appointment book and made a quick note. "Don't kid yourself, Nick," she said. "I'm not doing this to help you."

That Friday, he called in sick. Victoria was going away with her parents and sister to some family barbecue thing upstate for the weekend and she wanted to see him before she left. So he drove to Medford, a tiny suburban town an hour south of Hopewell.

She met him at the strip mall near her house. She'd told him she was never sure when her mother would be home and didn't want to explain his car in the driveway.

She was leaning against the brick wall of a 7-11, writing in a little notebook, when he pulled up. She wore a tattered black dress, combat boots with red laces, and the leather biker jacket two sizes too big for her, the sleeves hanging past her knuckles. Her hair was pulled up into several tall ponytails that stuck out in different directions. Two men in muddy jeans and workboots looked her over as they walked past, then mumbled something and laughed. She kept writing, head down, and didn't seem to notice.

He went over to her. "Hey."

She smiled and hugged him, then looked him up and down. "That's what you wore to the 321, isn't it?"

"I think so." He shrugged. He had no idea what to wear so had put on the same jeans and army jacket.

"Let's go." She took his arm. "You'll like this."

At the farthest corner of the strip mall, right next to the dumpsters, was a store called Splat. The window was covered with posters for the Dead Kennedys, The Cure, The Ramones and bands he'd never heard of. Inside, the Replacements played over loudspeakers, the singer rasping over spare, scratchy guitar chords.

The sleepy-eyed girl behind the counter looked up from a magazine. A floppy brown felt hat was pulled down to her eyebrows. "Hey. How were the Descendants?"

"They cut it short because there was a fight," Victoria said.

"That sucks." She went back to her magazine.

Victoria started pulling belts and chains off the wall where they had been hung on long nails. "You need this. And this. And they have clothes over there."

Lining one side of the store were racks of t-shirts and army pants and baggy shorts with lots of deep pockets and heavy shapeless dark blue pants like the ones janitors and mechanics wore.

Nick picked up a pair of baggy black pants with a strap that clipped around the legs. "What are these?"

"Bondage pants. You can take the strap off if you want."

Inside a glass display case were rows and rows of pins, each with the logo of a band. "It's every band I like," he said.

"Bird's got a million of them. She can't even fold her jacket she's got so many stuck on."

"If I wore them where I live, nobody would know what they were."

"I know. That's what's cool about it. And then every once in a while somebody will come up to you out of nowhere and say 'what's up' because they know you're into the same shit they are."

He wandered through the store, snatching up as many things as he could carry. She flipped through the records in a bin in the corner. The girl behind the counter put on the new Henry Rollins solo album. Nick glanced over at Victoria, about to tell her this was his favorite new album, but she was already whipping her head back and forth to the music. Her hair came loose and fell around her face and they both laughed.

"I want to live here," he said.

The girl behind the counter let out a snorting laugh.

Finally, he dropped all the stuff at the cash register and pulled a wad of bills from his pocket.

"Whoa," Victoria said. "You have money."

"The only good thing about having a job."

"I have one too. But it's in a record store." Victoria and the girl behind the counter exchanged sympathetic glances.

"What do you do?" the girl asked Nick.

"Accounts payable accounting for a software development firm." It always sounded like gibberish when he said it out loud.

She stared at him blankly.

"He's a total sellout," Victoria explained.

Outside, Nick said, "I am not a sellout."

They were walking along the sidewalk in front of the stores. He carried two overstuffed plastic bags and she'd linked her arm with his.

An old woman came out of the hairdresser's. A man, probably her husband, held the door for her. They were neatly dressed in khakis and white sneakers and dark, oversized sunglasses. The woman looked Victoria over. "*Dear*," she said sweetly. "You could be so pretty. Why would you want to go and do that to yourself?"

Victoria patted Nick's shoulder. "But my husband loves it."

The old man shook his head at Nick in bewilderment.

"Have a nice day," Victoria said with a wave. She was smiling and giggling.

"That was so rude," Nick said. "Who asked for their opinion?"

"Whatever." She'd stopped smiling. "That's nothing compared to the shit I hear in school."

She led him down a narrow alley that ran between the storefronts and the 7-11. "Let's go down here."

At the end of the alley the pavement ended and the ground dropped steeply to a ditch filled with soda bottles and beer cans and ripped-up newspapers. Beyond the ditch was a thick clump of trees with a dirt path winding through them. "Jump across," she said.

They walked along the path until it stopped at a narrow, fast-moving creek. "You know," Nick said. "You don't seem like somebody in high school."

"One more month. I can't believe it will finally be over. I get so much shit every day. From *everybody*."

"At least you have your friends with you, right? Those girls from the club."

"We go to different schools. I met them at the shows." She sat down on a log alongside the creek. Handfuls of cigarette butts were half-buried in the dirt around her. "Except for Rat," she said. "She's in my grade. Everybody knows by now I'll smash a cheerleader's face in. I don't care. But Rat is this tiny, chubby thing. So sweet once you can get her to talk. She hides in the library as often as she can. She gets it worse than I do."

"That's where I used to go. The library."

"Why? Who was after you?"

"Nobody. But I was hiding anyway."

"That's messed up."

He smiled grimly. "Now I hide in a cubicle."

"I'm not hiding. I'm not changing. People will just have to deal." She stared at the creek, elbows on her knees, shoulders hunched forward. Sometimes she looked very small.

"Where are we?" he asked.

"This is where I go. If you hop over the creek that path will take you right to my street."

He sat down on the log next to her. Victoria pulled a bottle of 7-Up out of her jacket pocket. "Want some?"

"Sure."

"Sorry it's just soda. My parents are very possessive with their liquor cabinet."

"That's OK." He took a sip and handed it back. They sat and watched the creek. The water was shallow and ran quickly over the smooth, round rocks on the bottom.

"Why are you so quiet now?" she asked.

He shrugged. "I'm always quiet."

They'd talked on the phone every night earlier in the week. About their favorite bands, about the songs that described their lives better than they ever could themselves. About razor blades and shotguns and sleeping pills. About guidance counselors and therapists and psychiatrists and psychologists, about school hallways and lockers and corporate conference rooms and cubicles. It had been easy then, sitting in his dark bedroom, the only illumination the green glow of the buttons on the telephone, listening to her soft voice, the careful way she spoke, as if she held each word gently in her mouth for a moment before releasing it. But this was different. It had been so long since he'd sat beside someone. He felt clumsy and unprepared.

She tossed her empty bottle into the creek and watched it float over the rocks. A web of low-hanging branches snagged the bottle and held it in place, the current rippling around it. He bent over and untied the laces on his scuffed black Reeboks.

Victoria said, "Please tell me you're not going to put your feet in that water."

"No. I just hate these. They make me look like a kid." He yanked off the sneakers, pulled a big shoebox out of one of the bags and opened it. "What're these called again?"

"Engineer boots."

"They're cool."

"Yeah. But Doc Martens are better." She knocked on the tip of her boot with her knuckles. "Steel toes."

Nick pulled on the boots. They were black leather, with thick soles and heavy straps around the top and the ankles. He stood and walked around, feeling like bricks were strapped to his feet. "I'm going to wear these every day of the week."

She raised an eyebrow. "At your job?"

"I know. They already give me crap for not wearing the right kind of ties."

"Seriously?"

"Well, nobody really says anything. They just roll their eyes and make faces. Then they make fun of you behind your back and you hear about it from somebody else a few days later. That's how you're supposed to communicate."

"That's just sad."

"It's getting worse there, too. I don't know why. They're constantly checking our work and ask us about our stupid 'career path.' Everybody's trying to screw everybody else over, just to make themselves look good. It's pathetic."

She tugged on a lock of hair that had fallen between her eyes. "I'd go insane there. I'd stab somebody."

"You feel stupid getting mad though, because it's all so petty. But the pettiness is what makes me mad. You can go all day without hearing one sincere word." Nick stomped in the dirt, enjoying the dull solid thump his boots made. The office seemed so distant today. He felt like he was talking about someone else.

She motioned for him to sit next to her. "You should cut your hair." She put an arm around him. "You'd look good with a short 'hawk. Maybe just an inch high."

"I don't know."

"You could get Bird to do it. She does an excellent job."

"Is she a hairdresser?"

"No." She giggled. "She just likes cutting things."

He smiled. Victoria always laughed in quick exuberant bursts, like her own laughter had taken her by surprise. "What's with her? When you guys left the show she was kind of giving me a hard time."

She shrugged. "She's like that."

"It was weird."

"Don't let it unnerve you."

"It didn't bother me. It was just weird."

He decided to stop talking about it. He couldn't describe now how he'd felt. The blank expectation on Bird's face, and no idea what he was supposed to do about it.

"She hasn't made up her mind about you," Victoria said. "She doesn't know if I should trust you."

"How would she know anything? About me, I mean."

"She doesn't. She looks out for me though. Somebody has to."

He leaned into her. She ran her hands through his hair while they kissed. "Look." She pulled up the sleeve on her jacket and showed him her wrist as if presenting him a gift. "It's like I said. You can barely see them."

He lightly touched the narrow pink scars. "How long ago was it?"

"A year."

"Does it feel like a long time ago?"

"Usually, yeah. I can still remember everything clearly. But it feels distant. A lot of stuff has happened since then."

They stared at the creek.

"Sometimes I feel like I'm still back there," Nick said.

"But you're not."

"I know that. But don't you feel . . ." He shook his head and shifted.

She waited.

"Don't you feel like part of you never came back?"

She nodded, watching the creek. "Yeah," she said, as if the answer were obvious.

He stared at the water. "There's a creek like this that runs by my house. It goes through all my neighbors' backyards. There was this spot about three houses down. Since it was dark and nobody would see me under the trees until the morning, I figured somebody walking their dog would call the cops. Spare my parents a little bit. But then I threw up all the pills. Somehow I got back home. I was so sick I finally had to tell my folks what I'd done."

"That's when you went to the center?"

"Yeah, eventually. But first it was to the doctor, then a psychiatrist, then a psychologist. Then the center. And after that a therapist for a little while."

"I got along great with my therapists. They were always telling me about their day, their kids, their weekend plans."

"That doesn't sound like therapy," Nick said. "That sounds like plain old conversation."

"I know. I didn't get it either."

He continued watching the water coursing over the tiny rocks. He thought about the center often, that moment in the lobby when his dad, indignant, had held the door open and beckoned to him to leave. Nick had hesitated, glancing around at the other kids. Some were bent over in their seats staring at their own clasped hands. Some scowled. Some sat bolt-upright with arms tightly folded. He'd recognized himself in the awkwardness and fear and aimless anger.

He belonged there. So when he followed his dad out the door he had felt like he was abandoning them. A stupid thought, he told himself later. He didn't know them, they didn't know him. But still, he recalled that moment often.

He turned to Victoria. "Remember when you asked me about it, that first time at the club?"

"Of course. It wasn't that long ago."

"Why did you say that to me?"

"I don't know. I just said it."

He pressed the heels of his boots into the dirt. "It really woke me up. Like somebody had shined a light in my eyes. I don't know where I've been the last five years. I've just been a passenger."

They leaned against each other, shoulder to shoulder, and didn't speak.

Finally, Victoria said, "Hey. I got something for you." She reached into the inner pocket of her jacket and pulled out a silver chain and a tiny padlock. "I was in a pet store near where I work and stole this for you."

She put the chain around his neck and fastened the ends with a click. "It's just like mine."

"Thank you." The metal links felt cold against his skin. He touched the chain. "Why did you even bother talking to me that night? I was nobody special."

"I just knew," she said.

"Knew what?"

She kissed him on the mouth. "Why did you let me talk to you?" she whispered. "Or let me take you outside?" She looked him in the eye, their faces inches apart, with an unwavering sadness in her gaze, like some mournful thought was fixed there and would never leave. "Well?"

He wrapped his arms around her and buried his face in the hollow of her shoulder. The collar of the leather jacket was cool against his cheek. They stayed that way for a long time, the creek chattering, traffic humming across the highway in the distance.

"Before my mom is done with work," she said.

"Yeah?"

"I want to take you home."

"All right."

"And then I want to take you to my room, and tie you to my bed, and scratch you until you bleed."

"All right," he said, after a long while.

"Don't fight it," she said. "Just let me do what I want."

They were naked. Nick lay on his back, Victoria straddling his hips. She caressed him again and again, but each time he became fully excited she'd stop and drag her fingernails deeply across his belly and along his ribs. He twisted and squirmed, wrists bound to the headboard by leather belts. Gradually, eventually, he could not tell the difference between pain and excitement and when she pulled her hand away his entire body quivered waiting for her touch. She bit into the lean muscles of his chest and he shuddered and finally gave in, feeling himself fading away. No will of his own. He was whatever she did to him.

She grinned. She bent forward, so close he felt her breath on his lips. Her white hair fell around her face and brushed against his cheek. "And you thought you weren't going to like it."

She reached down and guided him into her. He rocked his hips up and down, slowly and then more quickly, and she moved with him, closing her eyes and arching her shoulders back. Her lips parted in a moan and her face softened. The look of mourning that was always there fell away like a dropped veil. She opened her eyes and smiled, blinking against the strands of hair that had caught in her eyelashes.

"I love you so much," she said, eyes so pale she looked almost blind.

The bedroom gradually grew dim, until only one small square slant of sunlight remained on the closet opposite the bed. The cramped room had barely enough space for the bed and a chest of drawers. Black lace curtains were pulled back from the single window. The shelves were lined with candles and stacks of cassette tapes. Against one wall leaned the canvas of an unfinished painting, only the shape of a female nude visible, sitting with head bowed, outlined in thick black strokes.

Victoria lay beside him. She had untied his wrists and he was lying on his back, arms around her shoulders.

"You hardly make a sound when you come."

"I know," he said.

"So quiet all the time."

He felt gawky and skinny lying there naked. He reached down and pulled the covers over them. "Who is this singing?"

There was a cassette playing in the tape deck on the floor. When she'd gotten up to put the tape in, he'd glimpsed in the fading light the pale roundness of her body: the wide curve of her hips, heavy upper arms, thick shoulders.

"Siouxsie and the Banshees," Victoria said. "I love them. This is their live album."

Over an insistent, pulsing bass line, a woman sang like a ghost, whispering and screaming at the same time.

Nick said, "I think that's how you would sound if you sang."

"I wish. I do sing sometimes."

She told him about the band she was in with her friends and how bad they sounded because they could never find any place to practice. He listened, but he felt as if he were watching himself from far away. Why did this always happen to him—this inevitable feeling of remove? With the girlfriend in high school, the friends he'd had in Hopewell, a distance had always expanded, unbidden, between himself and them. Now it was happening again. He'd lost himself with Victoria for a moment but now only felt the sting of the scratches, the weight of her arm across his chest, the dim, warm closeness of the room. Nothing else. It was like he could only go so far with someone before he was drawn back into his thoughts and then, from there, would have to watch himself go through the motions.

She was silent. Finally, she said, "I guess we're done talking."

"Sorry. I get like that sometimes."

He pulled her closer. Her skin felt cool. Why not stay like this, submerged in her bed, eyes closed, music filling their ears? He didn't want to get up and go out, speak or be seen.

"What time is it?" she said, lifting her head. "Oh. We better go."

He slowly released her. She pulled on a threadbare black sweater. He put on his jeans and t-shirt. The choke chain jingled whenever he bent over. He sat on the edge of the mattress to pull on his boots.

She sat beside him and rubbed his back. He stiffened. He was not sure what had changed inside him, only that it had.

Outside, a car door slammed.

He turned to her, head bowed, and buried his face in her chest. "I want to stay here."

She ran her fingers through his hair. "We can't. My mom's home."

In the driveway, her mother's Ford Granada was parked at an odd angle.

"Mom, this is Nick. Nick, this is my mom."

"Nick to meet you," said the tall thin woman with big sunglasses and curly, copper-colored hair. She laughed. "I mean, *nice* to meet you, *Nick!*"

"We're walking back to his car, Mom. It's over by the pizza place."

"You guys have matching necklaces. That's so cute."

Embarrassed, he put a hand to his throat. "Thanks."

"It's a chain, Mom. Not a necklace. I'll be back in a few minutes. Want me to pick up dinner while I'm over there?"

"Get something for you and your Dad. I'm not hungry." She dug into her purse. "Here's some money."

Victoria and Nick walked along the sidewalk past the boxlike houses that lined the block. Each had a square patch of front lawn behind a wire fence. His boots made his stride more forceful. He swung his arms as they walked.

"My mom's out of it most the time," she said. "It's how she deals."

"She noticed the chains, though."

"Of course." She laughed. "They're shiny."

They headed back along the trail through the woods. "She seemed nice though," he said. "I didn't know what to expect after all that yelling on the phone."

"It's still early. And my dad's not home yet."

They stepped over the narrow creek and walked up the dirt path that led behind the strip mall.

"What's the story with your folks?" she asked. "Are they together?"

"They are, but shouldn't be."

"They fight too?"

"No fights. Just these really long silences. Like for months at a time."

"I'd believe that." She nodded, as if confirming something to herself.

The strip mall was busy with cars going in and out. They hugged and Nick got into his Chevette.

"Call me later," she said.

"I will."

"I love you."

He lowered his gaze.

"So quiet." She cocked her head to one side. "Do I scare you?"

"No." He noticed small holes in her black sweater where her pale skin showed through.

"You don't seem very sure."

"It's not that."

She waited. He shook his head and sighed. It felt like he'd left part of himself back in her room. "You don't scare me," he said finally.

"You're not going to disappear, are you? Everybody I love disappears."

"No. I won't."

"It's OK if you want to. I'm serious. It's really OK. But tell me if that's what you're going to do. I only have one person in the world I trust so far and it would be really cool if you could be the second. We can look out for each other."

He shifted in his seat so he could look her square in the face. No one had ever spoken to him so directly and honestly before. "I'm not going to disappear. I promise."

They kissed goodbye and he drove out of the lot. In the rear view he saw her standing there, still watching, arms crossed, shoulders hunched forward. A car pulled up behind her, trying to turn into the space he'd just left, but she was in the way. The driver honked. She turned and stared the driver down for a moment, then walked away without a backward glance.

After a long ride in silence through the I-95 rush hour, Nick took the exit for Hopewell and slowed to a halt at the traffic light at the bottom of the ramp. He absently fingered the chain around his neck. Only then did he recall there was a tiny padlock holding the chain in place—and Victoria had the key.

5

YOU LOOK AT YOU

By the time he got home his parents were already in the living room eating dinner in front of the TV, his mother on one end of the sofa, his father on the other, each with an individual folding snack tray. His father still had his tie on. His mother's plastic office ID badge was pinned to her sweater.

"Your father picked up pizza," she said. "It's on the dining room table. Sit down and eat before it gets cold."

He froze in the hallway that opened onto the living room, startled. He was carrying the three plastic bags full of clothes and albums from Splat. He'd been thinking so hard about Victoria and what to do about the steel dog collar locked around his neck, he hadn't even noticed the murmur of the evening news as he came through the front door.

His parents stared at the TV, jaws moving. The floor-length beige drapes held the glow of the setting sun so the living room was suspended in wan yellow light. On the end table next to the sofa was his father's newspaper, as always, folded in squares during his ride on the train.

It took Nick a moment to realize he should speak, should make some movement. "I have to put my stuff down."

He went to his bedroom in the back of the house and dropped the plastic bags on the bed. Whenever he turned the dog collar swung then fell back, the steel links cool against his skin. He tucked it underneath his t-shirt. He didn't feel like explaining to his parents. Throughout high school, the slightest change in his behavior had brought frowns of worry. Whenever they found him daydreaming. If he slept too late on Saturday. If he got up too early for work, if he came home too late—anything could set off the exchange of furrowed glances. But they never said anything to him. Only frowned at each other as if in confirmation of something until now only suspected. He understood why they were like this, but he dreaded the sight of those creased foreheads. He wished he had a brother or sister, someone else to absorb all this concern and attention. A sibling who excelled in soccer or baseball, or any sport. Who could finish college. Someone whose potential wasn't always considered squandered, who always had a new, amusing story to tell. Not him—whose every day was exactly the same.

But over the last year, maybe from all the time he'd spent mimicking small talk in the office, he'd learned how to get along, stay beneath attention. It was simple, actually. Do what was expected of you, do everything right, and eventually you could efface yourself, be free from the scrutiny of parents, beneath the notice of people at work. It was easier that way. Like everything was happening on a movie screen he watched in the dark from the back row. At least, it had been easy.

But now, when he pictured himself pacing the muffled halls of the office in his baggy J.C. Penney plaid shirt and lopsided knit tie, he felt his plan had gone wrong. He'd accidentally transformed into someone else, someone he didn't want to be.

He adjusted his collar again and glanced in the bathroom mirror. The little padlock at the base of his throat made a lump under the shirt. He rubbed his eyes and sighed. He had no idea what to do about the dog collar. No idea what to do about Victoria, or if he even needed to do anything. He could still feel the naked weight of her, her warm breath against his lips as she'd bent over him, whispering.

He went back to the living room. The anchorman was saying, "... *but President Reagan stressed he had no knowledge that profits from arms sales to Iran were being diverted to the contras.*"

"That's why you called in sick?" his father said. "To go

shopping?"

"I have time left over," he said, which was a lie. He'd called out so often he'd lost track of how many sick days he had left. "I have to use it before the end of the fiscal year."

He picked up a snack tray from where they leaned in the corner and opened it. When he bent to set it in front of the loveseat, the farthest point from where his parents sat, the padlock slipped free and dangled under his chin, the steel links making a tiny tinkle.

"Oh God," his mother whispered. She looked away with a quick shake of her head.

"What," Nick said.

His father looked at him, then rolled his eyes over at his wife.

Nick went into the dining room, opened the box of pizza and picked up a slice too quickly. All the melted cheese slid off back into the box. He dropped the slice on his plate and stared down at dabs of tomato paste on the greasy cooked dough. Feeling about ten years old, he went back to the living room.

His parents exchanged glances. They seemed to be accusing each other of something. Nick kept his eyes on the TV. The anchorman was blonde, blow-dried, his face a smooth, tanned blank. Above his left shoulder hovered a picture of a handgun superimposed over a chalk outline of a body. Under this the words *Murder in the Bronx*.

They were watching the 6 o'clock news out of New York City. Even though Hopewell was ninety miles from the city, his parents always knew everything that was going on in New York. There were no New Jersey news shows. And Philadelphia didn't count, even though it was closer.

His parents had moved out of New York before he was even born, but growing up all he'd ever heard about was the West Side, Uptown, Penn Station, Grand Central. He would sit on the carpet with his green plastic soldiers while they watched the news or *Barney Miller* or the Yankees. When he was seven, they'd taken him to the Museum of Natural History. That was the only New York he'd seen for himself: a narrow slant of light between skyscrapers as he'd twisted his neck to look up and out of the window of the taxi cab. He'd never noticed the trash, the homeless, the triple X parlors. But that was all his mother had talked about on the train ride home, her face locked in an imprint of insult, as if it had all been done specifically to offend her.

He didn't understand any of it. Why keep talking about this place they never went back to anymore? For him, the city was just his dad's *Times* folded into squares, his wrinkled charcoal gray blazer, the black plastic briefcase with scraped corners. The city meant nothing to him, except as a reminder he was not in the center, that he had always lived on the periphery, irrelevant.

A commercial came on. A BMW passing a convoy of 18-wheelers on a winding mountain road. Classical music played. The woman in the passenger seat turned to the man driving, her long golden hair whipping in slow motion around her face, and smiled. He smiled back, the landscape speeding past in the background. Their faces somehow looked old and young at the same time, heavy and smug with middle age, but no wrinkles, as if their skin had been pulled tight and buffed smooth.

His father was staring at him again. "You have any idea how ridiculous you look with that thing?"

"I like it." He kept chewing. The pizza didn't taste like anything. "I'm tired of looking like everybody else."

His mother frowned. "People look like everybody else for a reason."

He took another big bite and chewed and chewed. The news came back on. A reporter with a microphone stood by a fountain outside a towering glass office building. Behind him people were filing out, carrying boxes. "*Many corporations are still struggling to recover from the effects of Black Monday, when the Dow Jones plummeted 508 points, the lowest level since the time of the Depression.*"

"I like it," Nick said, pretending to watch the TV with great interest. "I wouldn't have bought it if I didn't."

Back in his bedroom, he found a paper clip in the bottom of his nightstand drawer and straightened it. He went to the bathroom and leaned over the sink to get a good look in the mirror at the tiny padlock. With one end of the clip he poked at the hole in the bottom of the lock. It clicked against something, but stayed locked. Down the hall, the television stuttered as his father flipped through the channels. He must have already settled back in the couch, the remote control on his lap. That meant his mother had gone upstairs, with her cup of tea and her sewing kit.

Nick dropped the paper clip on the counter. "Damn it." It wasn't working. He held the lock between his thumb and index finger. With the other hand he pinched one of the links the lock was looped through. He twisted as hard as he could, but his fingers kept slipping off the smooth steel. He thought about cutting it, but the tools were all locked in the shed and that meant asking his father. He bowed his head and took a deep breath. How was he supposed to go to work with this thing around his neck? How was he supposed to go anywhere?

He ran his fingers over the steel chain, which glimmered and winked cheerfully in the bright lights above the mirror. He would have to see Victoria again, even though he wasn't sure he wanted to. All that intensity, that overwhelming need. Just thinking about it exhausted him.

He hooked his fingers underneath the chain and pulled it up over his chin. There seemed to be just enough slack to get it over his head. He bent over and slid the chain up the back of his head, but it got caught underneath his ears. Pressing his earlobes down with his thumbs, he managed to slide it further over his ears. The links bit into the sides of his face. There was no more room to get his fingers underneath the chain so he tried rolling it upwards. The chain tightened around his face, cold steel links pressing into his upper lip and along his jaw line. Cursing, he dropped his hands and straightened up. But the chain was stuck on the back of his head, the links twisted in his thick hair. It hung now like a bridle over his ears and under his jaw.

"You're fucking ridiculous," he said to the mirror.

In the late evening Nick sat in bed, his back against the headboard. All of the stuff from Splat was dumped out on his bed but he hadn't looked at it yet.

"So how am I supposed to get this chain off?" he said, leaning into his phone.

"Oh," Victoria said. "I still have the key."

"Yeah. You do."

"I'll bring it with me to the Murphy's Law show. You're going, right?"

"Yeah. But that's like a week from now."

"So? It looks good. And you've got all those cool clothes too. Now just do something about your hair."

"That doesn't matter. It's not like I can wear it everywhere."

"Why not?"

"Because I can't. It's not like I can wear this thing to work."

"I thought you didn't care about work."

"I don't." He sighed, remembering what she'd said to the girl at Splat about him being a sellout. How the two of them then exchanged such self-assured glances. As if they really knew him.

"So there's no problem," she said. "You have a whole new look."

"I didn't *ask* for a whole new look." The edge in his voice surprised him. A sternness that sounded like his father.

"You don't ask for anything," she said. "If nobody gave you anything you'd be happy with just nothing."

"You didn't even give me a choice."

"What're you so afraid of?"

"I'm not afraid."

"Then what are you so mad about?"

He shook his head. His anger was already crumbling. "I didn't say I was mad."

"You don't get it, Nick." Victoria spoke quietly and exactly, as if weighing each word. "I don't know why you don't get it. I liked the idea of you having something from me, something solid like a chain. Something wrapped around you that you couldn't take off. It's a romantic idea. And you'd think so too if you weren't sick of me already."

"I didn't say I was sick of you."

"You wouldn't be so pissed off about the collar if you were sure you wanted to see me again. You would like the idea."

He rubbed his face, feeling the tender dents in his skin where the chain had pinched. He didn't feel mad anymore, just lost. "I don't know what to say. I don't know what you want me to say."

"It's not a test, Nick. Say whatever you want."

"But it is. You expect me to say something in particular. You have this idea about me that doesn't really exist. None of it exists.

You're living in some world in your head and you think I'm part of it now."

A long silence. He had stumbled somehow and could not right himself.

"I'll be away for three days." Her voice was flat, suddenly weary. "Otherwise I would drive up there and take it off right now for you."

"You don't have to do anything. I didn't say that." He shook his head. Why was it, whenever he spoke to her now, he fumbled every word? It had been so easy on the phone that first week, sitting in the darkness of his room, talking late into the night.

"Hello?" she said. "Still there?"

"I'm here."

"The silence is cool and mysterious in person, Nick. But over the phone, it's just silence."

"Sorry." He sighed. "Never mind. I'll see you at the show. I'm sorry for making a big deal about it."

Her voice hummed against the receiver. "There's a crease in my pillow. Like a little valley. From when you were lying in my bed. I don't want to smooth it out yet."

"I'm sorry," he said again. "I had a great time today. I don't want to make it sound like . . . I don't know . . ."

"Whatever happens, I'll always remember today and smile. No matter what."

"I know." He tried to soften the edge still in his voice. "Me too."

But he was home now, back in his bedroom, and what had happened with her, out there, seemed to have happened to somebody else.

"I better go," she said quickly.

"Oh. All right . . . are you OK?"

"Yeah. I just have to go now."

"OK."

"I'll think about you while I'm gone."

"Me too."

"Don't say things just to say them."

"What?"

"I love you," she said, and then hung up without waiting for a reply.

* * *

The next day, Saturday, after staring at the back covers of the albums he'd bought, the sullen, defiant faces of the bands glaring back at him, Nick made up his mind. He walked to the barbershop in the little strip mall in town. It sat between the dry cleaners and the hardware store, with a broad plate glass window in front. The blinds were pulled all the way up, the front door propped open with a plastic chair. Danny was sweeping up a small pile of hair with a broom in one hand and a dust pan in the other. He was older, dressed simply in gray pants and an untucked black short-sleeved shirt that hung like a half-raised curtain over his round belly. The dust pan had a long handle so he didn't have to bend over. He'd been cutting Nick's hair since he was fourteen. Every time it was the same: a quick trim and ten minutes of small talk.

"Be right with you, Nicky," Danny said. He had faded tattoos on both forearms: a ship's anchor on his left, and *US of A* on his right. The thick muscles of his arms twisted as he swept, the tattoos stretching and creasing.

It was late morning, and sunlight slanted in through the big window, glinting off the polished metal arms of the chairs. The two other barbers, both stooped, bespectacled men with silver hair, watched Italian soccer on a TV propped in the corner. A small boy sat in one of the barber's chairs, kicking his feet and grinning. His father kept an eye on him from one of the plastic chairs set under the front window. "Don't be scared."

"I'm not scared," the boy said.

"How you doing, Nicky?" Danny brushed off an empty seat with his towel and Nick sat down.

Danny was the only person who ever called him Nicky. He draped the green plastic apron over Nick and fastened it in the back. "The usual, right?"

"I want it spiked."

"Spiked?" Danny raised his chin and looked down at Nick through the bottom half of his bifocals. His blue eyes were big and watery behind the thick lenses. "You mean like that *Top Gun* thing?"

"God no," Nick said quickly. "Just spiked."

"Still not getting you, Nicky."

So he tried to describe the haircuts he'd seen at the 321 Club and on the backs of the album covers. He turned halfway around in his chair to look at the barber directly. Danny watched him, one eyebrow raised. Nick moved his hands around his head as he spoke.

The barber shop got very quiet.

Danny swung Nick's chair around so he was once again facing the mirror, then stood behind him, hands raised, a spray bottle of water in his right hand, a long comb in his left. He spritzed Nick's head a few times. Under his breath, he said, "Now why the heck would you want to do that."

He ran the comb through Nick's hair. Wet and straight, his hair fell down to his eyebrows. Danny caught the tip of his tongue between his teeth and eyed Nick's head. With a slight press of his fingertips, he bowed Nick's head so that he was staring down at his lap, then rolled down the collar of his shirt.

"That's a hefty piece of jewelry you got on there," Danny said.

"Oh. Yeah." Nick had worn an old polo shirt, an apple red one with a tiny Izod alligator on the chest. The only thing he had, not counting his dress shirts, with a collar that he hoped would cover the dog chain. "This, uh, girl gave it to me."

Danny raised an eyebrow at Nick in the mirror. "Oh yeah? You got a girl?"

"Well. Kind of, yeah."

The scissors started snipping. After a while, Danny said, "I guess she can't be too exciting if you don't feel like talking about her."

"No. It's not that. It's just . . . I don't know." He lifted his head. "You're spiking it, right?"

"Hold still." Danny combed down the side of Nick's head, snipping off the ends as he went. "Let me even things out first. Then you can tell me about this spike business."

He continued methodically measuring and snipping. Nick's hair fell away like dark feathers, dropping down the lime green apron and gathering in the cradle it formed between his legs.

"Yeah, well, women are tough," Danny said thoughtfully. "A real mystery."

He put down the comb and scissors and picked up the electric clippers. Whistling tunelessly by blowing through his teeth, he removed the plastic blades from the clippers, picked up a longer set, and snapped them on.

"Don't worry, Nicky," he said. "You're a good-looking kid. Just got to talk more. You'll be all right."

"Wait. This is the part I want to stick up. Like, right around there. So it can't be too short or it won't . . . it won't, you know, stick up."

"Put your hands down. You're making me nervous."

"I just wanted to make sure . . ."

Danny flicked on the clippers and ran them up the back of Nick's head in one brisk motion. They rattled in his ear like an old car. Nick felt a cool breeze against his scalp.

Danny frowned down at him. "So, 'spiked.' You mean sticking up?"

"Yeah. You know, in spikes."

Danny finished running the clippers up the left side. "I guess I got something for that."

He picked through the cans of hairspray and shaving cream on the counter below the mirror, still blowing air through his teeth. "Oh yeah, here we go."

He chose a small round jar of white paste and held it at arm's length, squinting at the label. "Goddamn bifocals."

He turned the jar around and examined it more closely, reciting softly to himself, "'Place a dime-sized dab in the palm of your hand . . .'" then read the rest in silence.

"Huh." He shrugged, screwed off the cap and scooped out a large gob of the paste with all four fingers. He rubbed his palms together, then patted down Nick's head with quick hard slaps.

"Got any left over, we can simonize your car with this stuff," he said, laughing.

Nick clenched his jaw, head bouncing with each slap. Danny worked the paste into his hair. The man's fingertips were like steel points. He tightened his neck muscles and tried to resist, but by then his head was throbbing. He sank slowly into his seat.

"Stop moving around so much, Nicky." Danny picked up a small towel and wiped his hands.

Nick's hair was wet and splayed out in all directions. "That looks good!"

"Very funny. I'm not done."

"No. I mean it looks good just like that."

"You serious?"

"Just make it stick up some more right here. In the front."

Danny squinted at him in the mirror. "You're a riot. You look like a damn river rat. How you gonna take out your girl looking like that?" He picked up a brush with short, stiff bristles and a wooden handle that fit in his palm. It looked like one Nick's father used to shine his shoes. "That's what I call them. 'River rats.' Know who I mean?"

"No."

"You know what I'm talking about. Those ugly kids you see at the mall. With their hair all sticking up like crazy Indians?"

"Mohawks."

"Whatever you call them. Ugly as rats. No self respect. Somebody should sweep their asses into a dumpster and be done with it."

Nick looked down at his hands, remembering how at the Descendants show, the one that had been shut down early, two cops had dragged a skinny kid by his elbows across the parking lot. "*I'm not resisting!*" he'd screamed. "*I'm not resisting!*" His day-glo orange mohawk had split in half, two pieces flapping like cracked branches around his ears.

Danny ran the brush through Nick's hair over and over again until his scalp burned. With every pass of the brush the hair flattened out then sprang back up, each time getting smoother and straighter.

"The top doesn't have to be even," Nick said, his voice fading. He could barely hear himself over the Italian soccer game.

"Sure it does. Think I'm gonna let you walk out of here half done?"

Danny came around in front of him and crouched, gauging the length of his sideburns. He smelled like Old Spice and Listerine. He picked up the electric clippers. "How you want the sideburns?"

Nick thought for a second. He tried to recall the back cover of *Wild Gift*, the bass player with the sullen slouch, the back cover of *Walk Together Rock Together*, the band lined up against a wall, but no images came. Why hadn't he thought to bring it with him? He tried to remember the guys he had seen at the 321 Club. But his mind was a blank. "I'm not sure," he said, just as Danny ran the clipper down past his ear, trimming the sideburn clear off.

"That'll work," he said, finishing the other sideburn.

"I was hoping for longer," Nick said, sighing.

"Ah, they grow back quick. Just trim them when they come in." He picked up a shaving brush and batted the loose hairs off the back of Nick's neck. "There you go! High and tight. That's what they call that."

He undid the apron and shook the hairs out onto the floor. Nick stared at the mirror. His head was shaped as square as a table top, the crown of his head as even as a yard that had just been mowed. "Wow," he said flatly.

Danny shrugged. "Took me a second to figure out what you meant. Then I remembered all those guys that come in from the high school. Varsity soccer. Good kids. Big as houses. It was their last season together so they all got the same cut. I had them lined up like an assembly line."

Nick slumped back in his seat. Now, with most of his hair gone, his face looked elongated, and too pale.

"You doing any sports this year, Nicky?"

"I graduated. Almost two years ago."

"Good for you! So, getting good grades in college, right? Meet any nice girls there?"

"I quit college. I've been working at an office for about a year now."

"Good for you, Nicky! That's great. Getting a head start on your career like that."

"Career," Nick stared down at his hands. "I hate my job."

Suddenly, he was talking about work, the futility and emptiness of it. He could not stop, spitting out the words breathlessly, as if trying to get a bad taste out of his mouth. "But maybe that's what I deserve," he said, finally looking up. "Because I'm such a sellout."

Danny had busied himself re-arranging bottles and canisters on the counter, eyes downcast, like he had accidentally opened a door on someone's bedroom while they were undressing. He hung the apron on the wall and picked up a broom and the dust pan with the long handle.

"That's five, Nicky. If you don't like it I can fix it up in a few weeks."

Nick blinked, embarrassed by his blurted confession. The only sound in the shop was the soccer game. The little kid and his father were gone. "No, no. It's, it's OK." He rose and pretended to admire the haircut in the mirror. "It's good, Danny. A real good haircut. Thanks."

Locks of his hair ringed the floor around the barber's chair. Danny swept them into a pile, then swept the hair into the dust pan. He brought it over to the trashcan in the corner and lifted the lid. Nick dug into the front pocket of his jeans, thumbed through the folded money, and left a big tip on the counter.

"Thanks a lot, Nicky. See you next time."

Danny lifted the dust pan and flipped it upside-down. The remains of Nick's hair slid into the trash in a soft, soundless clump.

At home, his father was knee deep in a hole in the front yard, shovel in hand, a fishing hat pulled down to his eyebrows and the armpits of his t-shirt dark with sweat. He squinted at Nick. "The top of your head looks like a toothbrush."

Nick rolled his eyes. "What's the project today?"

Every Saturday morning he awoke to the sound of his father in the backyard, cursing at the mower that always took ten pulls to start. His dad worked on the yard every weekend—raking, pruning, planting, mowing—but Nick never noticed any big difference.

His father pointed, still panting. "We're taking that rhododendron out of there and putting it here."

"I have to go to the bathroom first."

"Well, hurry up."

His father bent again and shoveled with quick, hurried motions. Even though he started on the yard early in the morning and didn't do much else the rest of the day, he always worked frantically, in a flurry. It reminded Nick of the World War II movies on Channel 5 every Saturday afternoon: soldiers scrambling to carve out foxholes before the bombs fell.

Inside, his mother stood at the living room window holding a steaming cup of tea. She was still in bathrobe and slippers. "Are you going to help your father?"

"Yeah. In a second."

She took a tentative sip then turned from the window. "Hurry up and get back out there before he drops over from a heart attack." She glanced at the top of his head. "You actually walked down the street looking like that?"

Outside, his father had dug around the rhododendron and was now crouched beside it, pulling on the trunk. He looked up. "Oh, that's an improvement. Now you only look like a convict."

Nick had wetted his hair and patted it down. He picked up the shovel and angled its blade beneath the roots of the tree. He put one foot on the blade and pulled back on the handle with both hands, trying to work the roots free. The shovel was old, the handle polished smooth from use. After working all week touching only plastic pens and calculator buttons, he liked the feel of it, the wet coolness of freshly dug soil. But he wasn't going to tell his father that.

Grunting and panting, they finally pulled out the rhododendron and dragged it to the hole.

"God damn it," his father said. "It's not deep enough." He stepped down into the hole. By now, he was red-faced, sweat trickling down his neck even though it was only the middle of May. "Hand me the damn shovel."

Nick bent to pick it up and the tiny padlock hit him in the chin. He slid it around to the back of his neck.

"You ever take that thing off?"

"I do. It's not like I wear it every day."

"Well, maybe you should consider not wearing it around your mother." He drove the shovel into the soil and lifted it, but didn't seem to be paying attention and dropped the dirt right on the edge of the hole, instead of on the lawn. "It makes her . . . well, you know how your mother gets."

"Nervous."

"Concerned."

Nick watched the dirt sliding back into the hole.

"And none of us want to see her that way." His father glanced up with a slight smile.

"What?" Nick said. "Concerned?"

"You know what I mean."

"Why? Did she say something to you?"

"Of course not. But you can always tell." He leaned on the shovel. "And now you got this, I don't know what you'd call that sort of haircut. But you're nineteen years old—"

"This didn't come out the way I wanted."

"—a little late for a rebellious phase."

"I'm not being rebellious. I'm just trying to . . ." He wiped his hands on his shirt. His clothes were a mess of contradictions: steel chain dog collar, red Izod polo shirt, khakis with frayed hems, black thick-soled engineer boots. In fact, he had no idea what he was trying to do. He felt like he was slowly sliding down a hole, just like that tiny pile of dirt, into that same empty place his thoughts always returned to. He put his head down and stopped talking.

"Well, whatever it is," his father said. "You can make your own mistakes. But try thinking about her before you go out and do anything else weird."

He went back to digging, seeming more relaxed now, as if he'd resolved something. The strokes of the shovel were slower and stronger.

Nick put his hands on his hips. A car rolled past. The woman in the passenger seat waved. A neighbor, he guessed.

"Help me out of here," his father said, extending a hand.

He grabbed his father's forearm, feeling the cold sweat, the loose skin, and the soft muscle like wet cotton underneath. "We're almost done, right?" he said. "After this?"

They usually only talked about the yard, or what was on the television while they were sitting in front of it. Nick dreaded any other conversations, especially the ones about his mother. They felt like conspiracy.

Hairspray. Styling gel. Brylcreem (his father's). Mousse. Nick's hair was a flattened landscape, gleaming like an oil slick with all the chemicals he had dumped on it. No John Lydon vertical barbs. No Sid Vicious chaotic spikes. Nothing worked.

He stared hopelessly into the mirror. The cloud of hairspray slowly dissipated. With his hair shorn and plastered to his scalp, his face, always lean and narrow, was fully exposed for the first time in his adult life. Deep-set brown eyes a little too wide, with a pleading, hungry look. He pressed a palm against the mirror, covering his reflection, and felt the momentary comfort that came from disappearing.

In his dream the walls of the house had vanished. Their home was now a stage. It was night. They all sat in the living room, staring at the floor. His mother and father at either end of the sofa, Nick on the loveseat in the corner. No one spoke but each worried about the same thing: what would they do when the sun came up and everyone could see into their home? His father turned off the lamp on the end table. The moon draped its silver light on their bowed heads and bent shoulders. The phone rang. They did not move. It rang and rang. His father put his hands over his ears. The ringing was so loud it shook the floor and sent vibrations in all directions across the neighbors' lawns and down the street, shaking the trees, shuddering the walls of all the other houses glaring down at them.

It kept ringing.

He clawed for the phone in the dark. "Hello? Hello?"

"Nick, it's me."

"What? What's going on?"

"Are you all right?"

"I'm OK, Victoria. Jesus. I was asleep."

"I'm sorry."

"It's OK. I'm awake now." He took a deep breath and rubbed his eyes.

"I'll let you go back to sleep. I didn't know it was so late." Her words were slurring together, her voice unsteady. "I didn't have anybody else to call. Bird gets hassled if I call her house too late."

"Are you crying?"

"Yeah."

He heard muffled little gasps. She must've put her hand over the receiver. "Why? Where are you?"

"Upstate. Like I told you. The whole big family fucking reunion thing."

"Oh."

"I hate them. I hate them so much." She spoke in a whisper, breathing into the phone as she moved around. "They don't even talk to me anymore. They just stare and shake their heads. And they know I can hear what they're saying, but they don't care."

"So what h—"

"It's like I don't exist. And then my mom started on her scotch and sodas."

"What happened?"

"What always happens. It gets worse each time we're all together, though. Like they need me to be a sacrifice or something. I can't stand it. I don't bother anybody. I just want to be left alone." Her voice went distant.

"Vic? You still there?"

"I'm here. I almost tripped over something."

"Where are you right now?"

"In my aunt's kitchen. Everybody's asleep. I can't see a thing." There was a metallic clatter. "I'm trying to find some napkins. My face is all wet. My cousins are sleeping right down the hall so I can't turn on the light. It's one of those Architectural Digest kitchens for 'entertaining,' not for eating and drinking like a normal person's. Everything has to be just right, so there's nothing on the counters. And all these copper pots hanging down in the middle of it. I can see their shadows. They're like, like severed heads. And it's so quiet. I can hear every little creak the house makes. It's like being inside a crypt that smells nice—Ow!"

"What happened?"

"I hit my foot on a stupid cabinet!"

"Are you hurt?"

"It's not that. It's just . . . God I hate this . . . I wish I could just go . . ." She let out a long sigh. "Sorry. I wasn't going to call you at all while I was here. But I didn't know who else to call."

"It's OK."

"I was going to say I wish I could go home but *no* I can't do that because that's where *they* live. Where am I supposed to go?"

"It'll be all right, Victoria."

He knew he should say something more, but there was only a big empty space in his thoughts. He listened to her crying, a quiet stifled whimpering that seemed inexhaustible. He laid an arm across his eyes, awed by the intensity of it. Then he held out his hand in the dark, as if he could touch her.

Finally, he said, "It's OK. I'll stay on the phone for as long as you want."

She sniffed a few times, then sighed again.

"Wouldn't it be great if every person in the world was blind? If everybody was blind, we'd all have to be nice to each other."

Sunday evening. Nick paced his room, listening to the last song on the first side of the Black Flag album he'd bought with Victoria. When it was over, he lifted the needle arm and played the song again. The guitar whined like a drill, pitching back and forth between two notes, while the singer howled, deep-throated, *"I'm the swinging man and my feet never touch the ground."*

The song ended and he lifted the needle and turned off the player. Scattered across his bed were the albums from Splat, along with with a flyer the clerk had stuffed in his bag. It had 321 in bold across the top, and beneath that, in crude block letters: *The Necros and The Dickies.* Below it, in a handwritten scrawl: *July 23 at the 321 Club. 7:00. $6.00.* Beneath that was a Xeroxed newspaper photo of a man in the passenger seat of a car, his head cast back, a jagged black bullet hole in his forehead. A police officer was bent over, peering through the windshield.

Below the photo, written in black marker: *Is the life you're leading the one you desire? Make your own decisions.*

He opened his bedroom door. The house was quiet. It was eight but nobody had called him to dinner. He walked down the hall into the empty kitchen and finally recognized the silence. His parents were fighting about something. He quickly made a sandwich out of some leftover chicken and ate it in his room, jaw cracking as he chewed.

There was laundry to do. And work tomorrow. He needed to iron a shirt, pick out a tie, and hope the tie and the stiff collar of his shirt would be enough to cover up the dog chain.

What a stupid thing to worry about, he thought. Screw it.

He put on the engineer's boots and his father's old army field jacket. The front pockets were now covered with the pins he'd bought at Splat. *7 Seconds. Sex Pistols. PiL.* He looked at himself in the bathroom mirror, pulled at his hair with his fingers. After not washing it in two days he could now get it to stick up in crooked blades. Glimpses of pale scalp were visible in the bathroom light. Chemotherapy patient, his father had called it.

He hopped the creek behind his house, then changed his mind and leapt back over. He didn't want to walk through back yards. He headed down the tree-shrouded main street towards Hopewell's one traffic light. The song was still in his head. *Feeling no pain, no pain.* The stiff heavy boots slowed his step to a long, steady stride over the uneven stone sidewalk. He walked alongside a long iron fence, behind which sat the cemetery, one of the biggest tracts of land in the center of town. On the other side of the wide, straight street shops were shut up for the night. An 18-wheeler rumbled past, shifting gears with bellowing coughs as it slowed through town. From down the street, heading in his direction, came a group of men. The growl of the truck's engine subsided and he heard them laughing.

A white car sped past. A girl in the back seat turned her pale face to him. He kept walking.

As the men got closer they grew silent. Their faces were in shadow, but Nick saw flannel shirts hanging out, hair cut short up top and flopping in waves down the back of the neck. A familiar look from his high school days. Their workboots pounded on the sidewalk, a hollow *clump clump clump*. He walked through them. No one said a word.

A minute or so passed. From a distance a man yelled "Faggot!" Then laughter. Nick kept walking. His stomach tightened and his legs felt like taut rubber bands. He waited, but nothing happened. No footsteps behind him. All the way to the traffic light, he didn't turn around.

I'm not hiding, Victoria had said, her shoulders hunched forward, looking brave and frightened at the same time. *I'm not changing. People will just have to deal.*

He clenched his hands into tight fists. He would walk all night, all over town. Those guys would not stop him. He turned down a side street that was dark and still beneath the shadows of low-hanging branches. Funny that they'd waited to get far away before saying something. What did they see that had scared them? His stride lengthened, his heavy boots beating an uneven rhythm on the cracked and crooked sidewalk. His baggy army jacket swayed and the lock on the dog chain bounced on his chest. The tiny impact of metal against bone with each step.

No pain

No pain

He liked how it felt.

6

INDECISION TIME

Sunday, late afternoon. The sun dipped behind the 321 Club and the long square shadow of the building stretched across the cratered parking lot. Nick leaned against the trunk of his car, hands in the pockets of his jeans. He had on a Black Flag t-shirt and the new boots. He hadn't washed his hair for four days and he felt like ants were burrowing into his scalp. But at least now it was sticking up a little bit.

The doors of the club had just opened. Some people were going in, but he wanted to wait for Victoria so he could talk to her outside. He'd left something undone—he wasn't sure exactly what—but maybe when he saw her he would know what it was he wanted to say.

He'd only talked to her once the entire week, calling from work, and she sounded distant, her voice flat. Bird was there, yelling at her in the background to hurry up. They were going to the record store.

"I wanted to see how you were doing," he said. "Now that you're home."

It was the end of the day. Tina and Sharon were packing up, banging their metal file cabinets closed, laughing and chatting.

"I'm home. Same as usual. I just have to deal."

"I'm sorry I wasn't much help. You know, when you called the other night."

"You listened, Nick. That was plenty."

He heard Bird shouting. "Yo! We gotta go, Prettyboy!"

"What did she call me?"

"It's your nickname," Victoria said.

"I don't know if I like it."

"It's because you're not all hard like the other guys at the shows. We have to get going, Nick."

"It's OK. I have to meet with my boss now anyway."

Then she said, very quietly, "It was cool that you called me. Thanks."

For a moment, she sounded like herself—her voice soft and careful—but later, he thought maybe she had only been whispering so Bird couldn't hear.

As soon as he put the phone down, Deborah appeared in the entrance to his cubicle. She motioned to him with a curt wave and he followed her into her office.

She stood over her desk and pinned one long red fingernail on the job description she'd asked him to write. "This is the best you can do?"

"Yes." He touched his throat, checking that the shirt collar still covered the bulge of the choke chain.

"I find that hard to believe." She shook her head. Her gaze kept moving to the top of his head then snapping back down. "And I have to get these things upstairs right away so I'm not going to go over it again with you."

"I'm fine with it." He tried to make his voice neutral, but it came out sounding sarcastic.

"At least Tina and Sharon know to play the game, Nick. Their write-ups were complete bullshit but at least they did them, *and* did them on time. At least they did what they were *supposed* to."

"But why does it always have to be bullshit? Why is it OK to merely do bullshit?"

Deborah raised one eyebrow, either momentarily interested, or just startled that he'd actually cursed. "I don't know what your problem is. You could have it so easy. Just do what you're supposed to do."

"But everybody does that. Even though they all think it's stupid and pointless. Nobody speaks up, nobody says anything, and then all this stupid stuff gets this, like this momentum of its own. And suddenly nobody's questioning anything because nobody else is questioning it and they don't want to be the only ones to speak up. So we all end up doing stuff none of us see any purpose in."

His boss sat and opened her appointment book before he'd even finished. "I have absolutely *no* idea what you're trying to say." She shook her head so fiercely her dangling gold earrings swung back and forth. "But I have to ask . . ." She leaned forward and in a quiet but fierce whisper said, "What the *hell* are you doing to your hair?"

Now, outside 321, three guys and three girls a few cars down from him, all around his age, were laughing and talking. The girls wore thick-soled black boots and heavy leather jackets that made them look tiny and thin, like kids playing in grown-up clothes. The boys wore t-shirts with the names of bands he hadn't heard of, and combat boots with chains and bandannas. Their car radio was tuned to WTSR, the college station out of Trenton. The woman DJ with the quiet purring voice was on. "*Laurie here, giving you the best in hardcore music. In about ten minutes, doors open for the Sunday matinee at the 3-2-1 in lovely downtown Trenton, New Jersey. Murphy's Law and War Zone.*"

She didn't talk like the DJs on the rock stations. No exaggerated inflections. No rehearsed enthusiasm. Just a soft blur of words spoken quickly and evenly. "*Up next . . . I dig the name of this band, because—it's a long story—but I hate squirrels. From Louisville, Kentucky, this is Squirrel Bait, with "Kid Dynamite."*"

The DJs on TSR and PRB, the station out of Princeton, always said where the bands where from. *7 Seconds, from Reno, Nevada. Boston's own Gang Green.* None of the Top 40 or rock stations did that. The songs on those stations were presented like microwave dinners, as if they hadn't been created or evolved from anything, as if they came from nowhere and had always just existed.

The car speakers blasted a hardcore song he didn't recognize. The music sounded like buildings collapsing, imploding, tumbling inward. The drums were a jackhammer blur. The singer sang like the inside of his throat was in tatters. One of the boys beside the car jerked his shoulders side to side, his weight on one foot. Everyone laughed, except for one girl who shouted, "Stop it, asshole! I do not dance like that!" Then she started laughing too.

Nick bobbed his head to the song. This was his third show at the 321 Club. Music sounded even better when you heard it with other people who liked it too.

A rust-spotted Oldsmobile lumbered past. Nick straightened, then leaned back against his car again, trying to look relaxed. The people next to him turned off the radio, locked their car, and went inside. He crossed his arms and stood up. The Oldsmobile parked way in the back and then Victoria and Crow and two young men he hadn't seen before got out: a short kid in a tight-fitting zipped-up leather jacket and a tall, stooped blonde guy in a long black coat.

Nick leaned back on his car again. He put his hands in his pockets, then took them out. His mind had been quiet for a while, but now he was suddenly aware that he was here by himself, that his boots still looked too stiff and new. That he didn't carry himself the effortless way everybody else did, like Victoria and Crow and all of them, as if they'd been born looking like this, dressing like this, walking like this, jackets swinging, hands loose, heads lowered but eyes alert, gaze pivoting left and right, like stray dogs pacing down an alley.

Victoria's bleached blonde hair was pulled down in long strands around her face. Her skin was white and smooth—some kind of pancake makeup, he guessed—and thick black mascara made her pale blue eyes fierce and ghostlike. She wore a plain white t-shirt and a mini-skirt with black dots all over it, the biker jacket wrapped around her shoulders.

When he walked up, she placed her palm on his chest and pressed her cheek to his. He inhaled her rose-scented perfume and was back in her bedroom and he felt guilty all of the sudden for not being kinder to her. "I missed you," he said.

The young man next to her, the one with the jacket zipped up to his throat, snorted out a laugh. He had a pale, sullen face and messy, spiked black hair.

Victoria glanced up. "What happened to your hair?"

"You join the army or something, man?" the kid said, lip curled. He was acting as if they knew each other, but Nick had never seen him before.

Victoria pulled a tiny key out of her jacket pocket and unlocked the padlock for the dog collar. She slid the padlock and chain off his neck and held them out. "Now you're free." She put the lock and chain in the palm of his hand. "Bird can fix your hair. She's probably inside already."

Victoria and the dark-haired kid headed for the front door. The tall blonde guy and Crow passed. "Hi, Prettyboy," Crow said. She wore a long slinky black dress and high-heeled boots, hair pulled back in a ponytail. Her scalp was shaved bare along the sides of her head.

At the front door, Crow turned to Nick, "You're not going in already, are you? The opening band sucks."

He stopped in the doorway. Inside the alcove, one bouncer was searching the pockets of Victoria's leather jacket. The other was methodically patting down the dark-haired kid. The bouncer said, "Keep your feet on the ground in there, dipshit."

"Yeah, yeah," the young man said, rolling his eyes. With a sharp glance back at Nick, he followed Victoria inside.

"That's Austin," Crow said. "But we call him Sid, which is kind of obvious, I know. He went to school with Bird."

Nick squinted at her. "Are they together or something?"

"Well, you broke up with her, didn't you?"

"I did? I didn't even know we were going out."

"Next!" one of the bouncers yelled.

She looked Nick up and down. "You want to wait outside with me? Rat's going to bring our zine and we're going to try to sell them."

"Your what?"

Crow stepped back out into the sunlight and waited. She had green eyes and a long angular face.

A heavy hand fell on his shoulder. "Yo, asshole. You in or out?"

He went to the same spot behind the bar. No one was sitting on the footrest this time, but the heavyset guy with the thick glasses was there on the only stool. He glanced at Nick, nodded, and went back to his book.

"What's up?" the bartender said.

Nick ordered a Coke. On stage a lone man sat on a folding chair, bellowing a ballad, his elbows flapping as he worked the accordion perched on his lap. A small ring of people had gathered far back from the stage. To Nick's surprise, no one laughed, but they all stood half-facing the stage so they wouldn't look too interested.

The accordionist finished his song and mumbled thanks. A few people applauded. Over the PA the DJ announced the bands that would be coming to the club—it sounded like there would be several shows a week—then put on a Ramones song. Some people shouted along with the *Hey! Ho!*'s. The bar was getting crowded, but Nick didn't see Victoria and that guy Austin anywhere. Maybe they were in the back bar, maybe they had fake IDs, but he guessed it didn't matter. What was he going to say to her, anyway?

Crow and Rat circled around the bar, heading his way. Rat had a backpack slung over one shoulder. She grinned at him and ducked her head, hands thrust into baggy janitor pants, face hidden beneath long, multi-colored hair.

"You again," Crow said. She reached into Rat's backpack. "Take a look at this."

She handed him a thin pamphlet made out of Xerox paper folded in half and stapled. On the cover was a scratchy drawing and hand-lettering that read *this zine is an abortion.*

"Only a quarter," Rat said.

The drawing was a cartoon of a wrinkled fetus with big black eyes. Pasted alongside this was a photo of Nancy Reagan. The word balloon coming from the fetus's mouth read, *I can "just say no" right Nancy?* And Nancy Reagan's reply was, *That's right Mr. Fetus!*

"That's good," Nick said.

Crow looked up. "Thanks." She had been staring at his mouth. "I only did part of it. Bird did most of the work. She does a whole bunch of these."

Nick handed Rat a quarter.

"Holy crap," she said with a goofy smile. "Our first sale."

"Go try Mike Skin and those guys," Crow said. "I'm gonna hang."

"Thanks!" Rat said to Nick, then trotted off, bumping the people around the bar with her backpack.

"Good kid," Crow said, watching her go.

Nick nodded. They were silent for a while. The bar was nearly full with people now.

Crow turned to him. "Did you drive yourself here?"

"Yeah."

"Want to go out to your car?"

"What for?"

She lightly touched his hand. "Oh, you're so cute," she said, then turned and walked away, long ponytail and long dress swaying in unison.

A moment passed. Then he understood. He dropped his head and ran his hands over his face. He seemed to be stumbling through a fog and everyone else was a fast-moving blur.

Somebody came up alongside him. "What's your damage?" It was Bird. She peered up at his hair. "Wow," she said with a laugh. "Your coif's all fucked up."

"I'm fine, thanks. How are you?"

She leaned an elbow on the bar and waved to the guy with the paperback. Her denim jacket was covered with pins that caught the light whenever she moved. Underneath her jacket she wore a t-shirt with a cartoon dinosaur sitting in a swimming pool. "Victoria said you want my help."

"Where is she? I don't see her."

"I don't try to keep track of her in here." Bird's voice was husky, but strong, like a shout that had been blunted by too many cigarettes.

"She's with that guy that looks like Sid Vicious," Nick said.

"Austin. And don't tell him he looks like Sid Vicious. He hates that." She backed away from the bar. "You want my help or not?"

"My hair? What can you do? It's too short to fix."

"Sit." She pointed at the footrest. "It's just too even is all."

He sat down, back propped against the bar. The music on the PA faded out, which meant the next band was coming on. Bird knelt on one knee in front of him, pulled up the sleeve of her jacket and slid two fingers underneath her thick leather wristband. It felt private and quiet sitting under the bar. No wonder the girls did it. "It's kind of nice down here," he said.

Bird pulled out a square of paper, unfolded it and withdrew a small, flat, gleaming blade. She held the razor between thumb and index finger.

"What the hell," Nick said.

"Never know when you might need one of these."

"What're you going to do?"

She widened her eyes so that the whites were showing. "Ritual suicide!" Then she resumed her usual look of bemusement. "Put your head down. I'm just gonna fix the ends."

He bowed his head and felt her fingers tugging at his hair, surprised at how light her touch was.

"Why did you get your hair cut?"

"I don't know. Just felt like I should do it."

"I get that."

"I got a lot of noise about it at work. A lot of dumb jokes."

"That's probably a good sign. Look up." She squinted at the top of his head. "So you were trying to get their attention?"

"At work?"

"Yeah."

"No. I don't even want to be there."

"You do the nine to five thing, right? Five days a week?"

"Well, yeah. It's a full time job."

"So you spend like half your life there but you don't want to be there?"

"I don't have many other choices."

"Really."

The opening band started playing a dull, throbbing bass. "But I don't buy into any of it," Nick said. "I just do my job and leave." Guitars screeched and the singer howled. He raised his voice. "It's not my life. It's just something I do."

"Right. Eight hours a day, but it's not really you. Sure it's not the other way around?"

"I don't accept it. I don't go along with it."

"So why's the top of your head all Semper Fi? You wanted to shock the squares?"

"The barber—well, I don't know. Maybe. Maybe that was part of it."

"It's no big deal shocking a bunch of squares. That doesn't take any work."

"I know that."

Two guys worked their way past them to the other side of the bar. Bird ignored them as knees brushed her back. She seemed coolly unconcerned about everything going on around her—she wasn't even bothering to shout over the crappy opening act—but at the same time totally aware, too. How could someone be like that? Especially here.

"Putting on a new look doesn't make you any better," Bird said, eyes fixed on his face. "It makes you more like them. Look at Oz. He's totally hardcore and he looks like a fucking chemistry teacher."

"I don't know who that is."

"See? Everybody knows who Oz is. You should try actually, like, talking to people instead of just staring at everybody."

The band stopped playing. Someone applauded. A bunch of people booed. Nick shifted awkwardly. Who was this girl to judge him? She was jabbing at him with words. He leaned forward and planted his feet. He didn't know why, but he wanted to prove himself. "All I was trying to do was get that John Doe haircut. The one he has on the cover of *Wild Gift*."

"You gonna learn how to play bass too? Write some songs?"

"Oh, come on."

"Screw Exene?"

"I'm not trying to change into somebody else."

"Then why get a different haircut?"

No answer came to mind. They were both silent for a while.

Finally, Bird said, "And night falls on the desert . . ."

"Solidarity," Nick said without thinking.

He wanted to explain that ever since he'd heard that song on the radio driving home from work, that Rites of Spring song about choking on the past, he'd wanted to do something to demonstrate his loyalty, to show he'd made a decision, for once in his life.

Bird was already nodding. She knew what he meant.

"Is that why you did it?" Nick asked.

She lightly patted the top of her tall, spiky hair. "You mean beside that it looks so fucking awesome?"

He smiled. "Yeah. Beside that."

"I guess." She shrugged. "But it's not because I want to be part of some club. I mean, look around, dude. You got skins and you got Austin and that crew. And they all got their look. And Vicky's like a different person every time she goes out. But there's just as many norms and L7s, too. And they're just as into it as everybody else."

He shook his head. "I don't speak this language of yours."

She rolled her eyes. "You know who I mean. The 'everyday' people. Like, most of the people here if you really look. Getting your hair right doesn't mean shit. As long as you're into it, *for real*, who cares? I mean, you ever seen Hüsker Dü?"

"No."

"They look like the guys that work at Space Port. You know that arcade in the mall? But they kick ass live."

The club went quiet now, except for the chatter of the crowd. The opening band must've gotten booed off stage. The DJ announced War Zone was up next.

"And, hate to break it to you, dude," Bird said. "But *Wild Gift*'s like, five years old. John Doe's a cowboy now."

"You're kidding."

"Look at *See How We Are*. He's got long hair and a cowboy hat."

"I couldn't find that one."

"It's not as good as their earlier stuff."

"*Under the Big Black Sun.*"

"Shit, yeah! That's their best." She nodded. "That's the shit that'll get you through a long, dark night. Just keep playing it until the sun comes up." She frowned, studying his hair again. "Don't move."

Bird pulled and lightly cut at his hair with the razor. Her dark brown eyes and full, round face were like a little girl's, except for the steady, serious squint, as if she were deciphering a complicated puzzle.

"Stop staring," she said.

"I'm not."

"You're making me self-conscious."

He laughed. *"You* get self-conscious?"

"With those saucer plates staring at me, yeah."

"What's wrong with my eyes?"

"They're too big for your face." She sat back and folded the paper around the razor blade again. "I'm an artist. I notice shit like that."

"So I look psychotic, then?"

"No. Not psychotic." She slid the wrapped blade back underneath her wristband. "Desperate."

"Great. Now I'm the one who's self-conscious."

She laughed quickly. "Who're you kidding? You came in self-conscious." She licked her fingertips, reached over and ran them through his short-cropped hair. "It's totally fucked. Your barber like, napalmed it or something."

He bowed his head as she worked her fingers through his hair. There was a rip in her jeans, just above the knee, and a small patch of skin was visible, framed by tattered threads.

"It's better now though," she said, sitting back again.

"Thanks."

War Zone had started their set, the singer bellowing over a storm of guitars. The stage lights flashed on the wall behind Bird, red then yellow then white. Nick didn't want to get up yet but couldn't think of anything to say.

"So what did Vicky say to you?" Bird asked.

"When? Outside?"

She nodded.

"She said, 'You're free.'"

Bird nodded again, thoughtfully. "You broke her heart."

"We went on one date."

"You broke her heart, " she repeated slowly.

"How is that possible?"

"You." She pointed at him, then made a snapping motion with her fists. "Broke." She placed her palms on her chest and bowed her head in mock sadness. "Her heart."

"Stop saying that."

She went silent. She sat cross-legged on the floor, pondering something. People passed, walked around, almost tripping over her, but she didn't notice.

He said, "It doesn't make sense somebody could be that crazy about somebody else, that quickly, without any reason to think the other person feels the same way."

"Just because you can't imagine it doesn't mean it's not true."

"I can imagine it. I just don't see how it's possible in . . . in these circumstances."

"God, who talks like that? 'In these circumstances . . .'"

He scowled, angry at himself. Whenever he felt cornered he always lapsed into the way people talked at work. "So, I guess Victoria doesn't want to talk to me anymore."

"You broke—"

"Don't."

She smiled quickly. "What do you care if she doesn't want to talk to you?"

"I'm not heartless."

"If you say so." Bird's eyes were hard but bright.

"Where are you getting this from? You don't know me. I don't know you."

"You're right. I'm nobody."

"For somebody I talked to only once you sure seem to have a lot of opinions about me."

She shrugged. "Well, you already know all about me. Vicky told you, right?"

"She told me about the shows you guys go to, and the parties in people's garages. And how you met when those rednecks were harassing you."

"And what else?" She was staring Nick straight in the eye.

"What do you mean?"

Bird raised one eyebrow. "Huh. Surprise, surprise."

"Why? What did she tell you about me?"

"Like, everything."

"Like what?"

"*Ev-ery-thing.*"

And Nick knew from the look on her face exactly what she meant and he saw himself on Victoria's bed, tied down, squirming and naked like some frightened animal.

"Whatever Vicky does," Bird said. "It's like it doesn't exist for her until she tells me. Don't ask me why. That's how it's always been. And if I'm not home, she tells my answering machine. Which can be pretty fucking awkward if my mom gets to the machine first."

His skin burned, the heat rising up his neck and spreading across his face. "So I must be like a real joke then, huh?" he muttered.

"What?"

"Nothing." He got up quickly, bumping his shoulder on the edge of the bar.

Her mouth dropped open. "You're going?"

He tugged on the end of his jacket, shoved his hands in his pockets, then took them out. "I have to . . ." The awkwardness he felt in the parking lot had come back. That quickly. "I want to catch War Zone before they're done."

"Fine."

"How's my hair look now?"

"It's like, totally rad." A weak attempt at a Valley girl voice.

"Thanks for fixing it. I appreciate that."

"Sure." She shrugged, eyes downcast. "Whatever."

The bathroom was to the left of the stage, down a dim hall that ran behind a wall of speakers. No door, only a frame with empty hinges. He had to slip through the crowd along the edge of the pit to get there. Inside was one urinal filled with cigarette butts and dark yellow urine and a stall with no door and a toilet with a piece of paper taped to it that read *OUT OF ORDER tough shit ha ha*. No mirrors on the concrete walls, which was good. Hands on hips, he paced back and forth, recalling the way Bird had looked at him after that Descendants show, her long stare in the parking lot. Nobody had ever stared at him like that before: so openly and curiously. At work, they looked at him with narrowed eyes, like some errant invoice they didn't know where to file. At home, his parents eyed him the same way they'd look at the dirty dishes in the sink. Even Victoria didn't seem to really see him. More like she was superimposing him into some movie already running in her mind. But Bird, she'd seen him like he was a new person. Under the bar—all her questions not giving him any time to think, to doubt—he'd felt like he was inventing himself as he spoke, like he had a chance to become someone other than the obedient sellout. Instead, thanks to Victoria, he was already overshadowed by whatever image she'd conjured up for Bird.

Why did that bother him so much?

A young man poked his head in, a line already formed behind him. "Hey, you gonna do something or not?"

He went back out and stood in the back of the crowd, watching the end of War Zone's set. The singer paced back and forth across the stage, baggy army coat swaying. Sweat gleamed on his shaved head as he made a long speech about how much it had cost them to get down here from New York, how little they were getting paid, how capitalist greed was going to ruin the scene. People shifted their feet. A few jeered.

"But that's enough from me," the singer said. "What do you guys think? Let's hear from you."

He handed the microphone to a girl in the audience. She screamed, "Shut the fuck up and play!"

The crowd hollered and applauded. "OK," the singer said, nodding. "All right. I can understand that."

Nick worked his way back to the bar. Through the mob he glimpsed Victoria and Austin back against the wall near the DJ booth. Austin had his arms folded, nodding and sneering at someone. Victoria was shaking her head, mouth agape. Nick went up on his toes to see who they were talking to. It was Bird. She stood with feet planted far apart, jabbing a finger as she spoke. Victoria was a full foot taller, but she seemed to be cowering.

The band left the stage and the crowd broke up, moving towards the bar. Nick lost sight of the three of them. He slipped behind a group of skinheads heading towards the DJ booth, but then Bird passed him going in the opposite direction, head down, arms swinging.

"Hey," he said.

She stopped and turned. "What."

"Are you all right?"

"Are *you* all right?" She put her hands on her hips.

"Thanks for fixing my hair."

"You said that already."

People moved around them, bumping his back, grazing his shoulders. He shifted closer to her, trying to get out of the way. She didn't move as bodies slid past, jostling her elbows, shoulders knocking the back of her head. She didn't even acknowledge them. He had the inexplicable urge to hold up his arms on both sides to shield her.

"I didn't dump Victoria," he said. "I just couldn't deal with her and all that—that *need*. But I didn't abandon her. She never even gave me a chance to explain."

"It's your life."

"But I didn't abandon her like you think. I'm not the kind of person to do that."

"So? Do whatever you want." She cocked her head to one side and pursed her lips. Again, that bold stare. "What are you telling me for?"

"Because I care about what you think." He blurted the words before he'd even realized they were true. A warm blush rose in his cheeks.

Her mouth dropped open, then she rolled her eyes. "That's dumb. I'm nobody."

"You keep saying that."

"Because it's true. You sure you don't want to talk to Crow instead? You don't even have to converse with her first."

"What are you talking about?"

"Wow." She eyed him curiously. "You are slow."

"Look. Just don't judge me by what you hear secondhand. Victoria doesn't know me as well as she thinks. She has these ideas that have nothing to do with the real me."

"Dude." Bird scowled. "*You* don't even know the real you."

She turned and disappeared into a crowd of laughing young men in long t-shirts heading for the back bar. Someone bumped Nick hard in the back. He stepped to the side to get out of the way but got bumped again.

"Excuse me," he said, but the guy was still standing there. He turned.

"You're Nick, right?"

It was Austin. Pale skin with a row of red pimples across his chin like an angry scratch. Thick eyebrows and sullen, deep-set eyes.

Nick nodded. "Yeah."

They were about the same height, but Austin raised his chin so he could look down at Nick. "Victoria's with me tonight."

"OK."

"And she doesn't want to see you."

Nick felt the space around him opening up as people backed away.

"So, what're you gonna do about it?" Austin stared at Nick, who stared blankly back.

Finally, he realized Austin was waiting for a response. "Nothing." He had tried to say it defiantly, but it came out more like resignation.

Austin nodded and walked away.

Nick went to the back of the bar and sat on the only stool. His shoulders felt tight and stiff. His hands were shaking. He clenched fists and released them, trying to get the trembling to go away. The dance floor grew dense again with the shadows of people gathering in front of the stage. Some were already hopping up and down in place. Murphy's Law would be on soon, but he couldn't get excited about it.

"That's my seat."

What now? He turned. It was the fat guy with the thick eyeglasses, standing with his thumbs hooked into the pockets of oversized jeans. Nick looked him up and down, then snorted. The guy blinked from behind his glasses. Nick considered for a moment, then got up and moved aside. The guy pulled a slim paperback out of his back pocket and put it down on the bar. Then, bracing two hands on the bar rail, he hauled himself onto the stool.

"You could've told him, Neil," he said to the man behind the bar.

The bartender was dumping a bag of ice into a cooler. "I'm a little busy, Oz."

The guy opened his book and held it up close to his face.

So this was Oz. Nick stared. He had the exact same book at home: *The Myth of Sisyphus* by Albert Camus. The same edition even, with the big boulder on the cover. He leaned his elbows on the bar rail. He tried to recall that line about *the mind that desires . . .* but couldn't remember the rest. He still didn't understand much of that book, but something about it had felt true.

Across the bar, near the opposite wall where the DJ was perched in a raised booth, Victoria and Austin were kissing, her fingers clutching his neck, his arms encircling her waist. The stage lights went down and applause and cheers rose like the gush of a fountain. Bird and Rat ran past the bar—a flash of blonde spikes, followed by a blur of purple and green dreadlocks. The two small girls hunched over and tried to elbow their way into the crowd.

Crow slid up to the bar and waved down the bartender. She shot Nick a quick, mocking smile.

The lights came up on the band. "So what's up with that guy playing the big mushy thing?" the singer said. "Singing about love and shit. You're supposed to sing about beer and . . . and . . . I don't know . . . *beer.*"

He was small but muscular, with short-cropped hair, a t-shirt with the sleeves torn off, and tall black combat boots. "We just got back from this dumb-ass tour with people who don't get our kind of music. It's cool to be back in Trenton."

The crowd cheered. The bartender raised a fist as if in salute. The drummer counted off and the band launched into "California Pipeline." Nick recognized the quick snarling guitar immediately. The second song on the first side of their first album. One of the records Victoria had told him to buy when they were at Splat.

The crowd pressed forward, leaping high, hands outstretched, surging towards the stage. Whenever he played this song in his bedroom he wanted to knock down the walls with his bare hands, but right now he felt as heavy and dumb as a rock. He put a hand to his throat and ran his fingers along the base of his neck, fingertips tracing where the steel chain dog collar had been. He'd never talked to Bird before tonight, and in his mind he felt like he was still talking to her.

You don't even know the real you.

It was stupid, laughable, but if she hadn't walked away, what he would've said—what he wanted to say right now— was that she was right. That he wished he knew.

Beside him, Oz squinted at the stage, tapping a corner of the book on the plywood countertop in time to the beat. Across the bar, Crow sipped a soda while the tall blond guy in the long jacket talked away in her ear. The spot beneath the DJ booth was empty now. Victoria was gone. Bird and Rat, unable to break into the crowd, had started a pit of their own, dancing in place by twisting their hips and swinging their fists side to side. Austin surfed across the upraised hands of the crowd, pale arms flailing, t-shirt in tatters. The band thrashed around the stage, knocking over monitors and microphone stands. The hovering cloud of smoke held the white glow of the foot lights. To the right of the stage, the side doors were propped open with dented trash cans. A bouncer leaned against the door frame, thick arms folded, and yawned. Behind him, the sky was deep blue, the streetlights like stars. The wood bar top shuddered beneath Nick's hands with each thud of the bass. It was like the rest of the world had disappeared.

By the time he got home, there was already a message from

Victoria on his answering machine. He could barely hear her soft voice over the horns honking and voices shouting in the background. *I'm sorry about tonight, Nick. I really am. But Austin said you were cool. You didn't even flinch. Call me later.*

7

TOKENS & SIGNS I

Weary, body sore, eyelids heavy, Nick sat slumped in his cubicle, trying to lose himself in the comforting monotony of account numbers in tiny even columns, in dollar amounts that always balanced no matter how many ways they were divided up. Tina and Sharon and the other clerks were just coming in, their sleepy voices and the unlocking of metal desk drawers the only sounds in the early morning hush. Just enough noise to subdue the buzz of static in his ears from the show last night.

An older guy in a navy blue suit stepped softly into Nick's cubicle. Wire-frame glasses, thinning hair combed to one side, and a stern frown. Gary Somebody from Human Resources, he remembered, from the new-employee orientation last year. He glanced at the clipboard in his hands. His suit was so shiny and stiff it might've stepped off the rack on its own. "Nicholas?" he read off the clipboard.

"Yeah, Gary?"

Gary's forehead furrowed a plowed field. "I'm the man."

Nick squinted. "The what?"

"You're part of our workforce readjustment."

"Um. OK."

Nick waited for him to explain. Gary said nothing, but his eyes widened behind his glasses. Maybe bewilderment wasn't the reaction he'd been expecting.

"I don't know what that is," Nick said at last.

"Given the new circumstances under which the corporation is operating, certain adjustments in staffing have to be enacted as part of a workforce readjustment." Gary took a deep breath. "It was announced in the all-hands meeting last week."

"Oh. I didn't go to that." Nick had overslept that morning and spent most of the afternoon at the record store. "I was out sick."

"I'm sorry to have to inform you of this, but your position has been phased out. Get your things together and I'll walk you to the door."

He straightened in his seat. "I'm fired?"

Gary shook his head. "Your position has been phased out. You'll be contacted in the next three days regarding your severance package. There'll also be counseling available if you wish assistance through the transitional phase."

"You're kidding."

"Unfortunately, no." Gary folded his hands over the clipboard. "I'm sorry."

Nick rubbed his chin. "Huh." He grinned and shook his head. He felt like the victim of a prank he should've seen coming.

"Do you need a container for your things?"

He looked around. A box of blue ballpoint pens. A calculator and some extra rolls of calculator tape. Olive-green four-column pads. Data entry forms. A phone. "I don't really have anything." He stood to follow Gary, then stopped. "Wait."

On the wall outside his cubicle hung his nameplate. He slid it out of the square metal holder and put it in his back pocket. Gary bowed his head as if in mourning. They passed Deborah's office. Her door was closed.

Outside Tina and Sharon's cubicle, Nick said, "I have to say goodbye."

He poked his head inside. The two women glanced up. They hadn't spoken to him in more than a week, so he wasn't sure what to expect. "I'm gone," he said. "Laid off."

Their mouths dropped open.

"So I have to go right now."

They shook their heads. "That's so messed up, Nick," Tina said.

"I can't believe it," Sharon said. "This place is so screwed up."

"I know." He nodded. For a minute, it felt like old times, the three of them complaining, all talking over each other. Then Gary appeared in the doorway and Tina and Sharon lowered their heads and fell silent. Nick said, "Bye, you guys."

"Good luck, Nick!" they called after him.

It sounded like they really meant it. That startled him so much he felt a little hitch in his chest, a quick shortness of breath, as Gary walked him to the glass double doors that led to the rear parking lot.

"Once again," Gary said. "I'm sorry to have to do this. And we all wish you the best of luck in your future endeavors."

"Are they going, too?" Nick pointed at the clipboard. "Tina Matthews and Sharon Wisnewski?"

"I can't tell you that. That's not open for disclosure."

"Come on." Nick fixed his eyes on Gary's. He contemplated snatching the clipboard out of his hands.

Gary grimaced and fidgeted with the metal clip. "I'm not supposed to say." He had a round, puffy face and a patient, tortoise-like manner. Somebody's dad, Nick thought. "To be honest, I don't understand why you were tagged. But you're the only one from your department. I saw your file. Great marks. Spotless performance reviews. You'll do well at some other organization."

"I don't care about any of that," Nick said. "It's meaningless."

"I can understand why you would think that way right now."

"No. That's the way I've always thought. I just never did anything about it."

Gary opened his mouth to say something, then closed it. He nodded wearily and extended a hand. "Best of luck, young man. We'll be in touch in the next few days to finalize everything."

Outside, it was a clear, sunny morning. Nick sat in his car for a while before starting it. One by one, more people were escorted to the glass doors. A man in a suit—sometimes Gary, sometimes someone else—shook their hands, then they walked out, carrying a cardboard box. One man's box was stuffed so full he could barely see over it. A New York Giants pennant fell out, was snatched by a breeze and skittered across the parking lot. The man lumbered after it, stomping down on the nylon with one heel. He put the box down, picked up the pennant and tried to wipe off his shoeprint. "God damn it," he said, blinking, and carefully slipped it back into the box.

Nick drove around to the front of the building, heading for the exit. But it was even worse up there. He couldn't get past all the people milling in the lot. Some had started to leave, then stopped and gotten out to say goodbye to someone else. He put his car in park and got out, too. He didn't know anybody, though.

An older woman in a severe dark suit walked past, carrying a stack of folders under one arm. "I worked here fifteen years," she told Nick.

He grimaced and nodded, but felt a scowl pulling at his face. All around people were hugging each other, shaking hands. Somebody made a joke about it being too early to go to the bar. Others laughed without smiling. A few stood quietly, hands on hips, shaking their heads. So much surrender, Nick thought. Shouldn't they be breaking windows? Burning something? At least kicking in the headlights of all the BMWs and Mercedes in the executive parking spots?

More people came down the front steps. More hugs and tired jokes. Behind them, the glass face of the building gleamed like water in the light of the morning sun. Nick leaned against the open door of his car, head bowed.

"You guys are pathetic," he said, but nobody seemed to notice.

At last, he went home. He didn't know what to do next. He drifted from room to room in the empty house. He went upstairs and paced through his mother's sewing room, shaded and dim, then to his parents' bedroom, their king-sized bed neatly made, the off-white comforter tucked in so tightly the mattress looked like a slab of concrete bound in cotton. He peered out the front windows. Hopewell seemed bright and harmless during the day, the leaves of the maples fluttering in the sunlight, the porches empty. Somewhere, a lawnmower buzzed.

Downstairs, back in his room, his answering machine was blinking. He pushed the play button. It was Victoria. *You didn't answer your phone at work so I'm guessing you stayed home. Me too. Sorry about Austin. Don't be mad at me. I didn't tell him to do it. I'll try you later.*

He erased the message and picked up an album at random: *My*

War. Black Flag with their last singer, Henry Rollins. He put it on the turntable, tossed his shoes in the corner, and sat on the bed. The needle crackled for a second, then a buzzing guitar snaked over a shuddering bass line. Rollins howled, voice raw. Nick turned up the volume, then turned it up some more. Maybe it had something to do with the cheap production—even the label was crooked and it listed the songs in the wrong order—but he could not get the music to fill up his room the way his other albums did. Rollins' screams strained against a silence they couldn't overcome. It wasn't like the other hardcore albums: a singer's bellow leading a barrage of guitars, a wall of noise without one crack in it. Black Flag was different. They knew something. Rollins was screaming to keep the silence back.

He turned the volume up as far as it would go. It made no difference.

He was grateful when the phone finally rang.

Early Thursday afternoon they were in Victoria's bedroom, the black curtains drawn over the window. He leaned back against the headboard. She sat on the edge of the mattress, facing him.

"So, did you steal anything on the way out?"

"No," he said. "Just my name. So why aren't you at the record store?"

"I quit."

"You're kidding."

"Nope."

"Did you tell your folks yet?"

"I don't need to tell them anything. I found an apartment in Philadelphia. All they've been doing since I graduated is say how they're not responsible for me anymore. So now I'll prove they're right."

"What're you going to do for money?"

"I got a new job. In the city."

"Doing what?"

"Modeling."

"Really?"

She snorted. "Don't sound so stunned."

"Sorry. I only meant—what kind of modeling?"

She shrugged. "All kinds. They said whatever I feel comfortable doing. The pay's great if my pictures sell. I have to try it. If I don't like that I'll figure something else out. But I have to get out of here."

"I never go down to Philadelphia."

"It's only an hour. Maybe a little more."

"It always seemed like a different planet. Even when I hear there's a good show down there, I always write it off."

"I guess that means you won't be visiting me."

"I didn't say that."

"It *is* a different planet," she said. "It's not the suburbs. That's what I want." She lay down beside him. "You should move down there too. Break out of this shell you're stuck in."

"Not without a paycheck first."

"Right. Stupid money."

"What's your boyfriend going to say about you moving?"

She looked puzzled. "Who? Austin? I'm letting that boy go. He's an angry puppy. Do you know Mike Skin? He's part of the Crew."

"No."

"I kind of go with him now."

"Tell me what he looks like so I can see him coming."

She smiled. "You're safe. I won't let anything happen to you." She touched his arm. "We have to take care of each other. Even if we can't see each other all the time."

"What about Foreskin? Doesn't he take care of you?"

"*Mike* Skin."

"Pig skin?"

She sat up, face close to his. "Stop it. You sound like Bird."

"Sheep skin."

"Shut up." She put a hand over his mouth. He kissed her palm. She turned and moved over him so her hips were straddling his. She grabbed his biceps and pinned his arms down.

He squirmed against her weight. "Hey."

"What?"

"What's Bird's real name?"

Victoria chewed at her lower lip, staring down at him.

"Well?"

She bent and lightly bit his cheek, her breath warm and soft in his ear.

"Ask her yourself," she said.

At home, he continued to wake up at exactly six-thirty A.M. It made no sense. He'd never been able to get up on time for work when he'd had his job, but now every morning he found himself lying in bed, eyes wide open, while down the hall from his room, kitchen cabinets opened and closed, the coffeemaker brewed with quiet burps, spoons clinked against ceramic mugs, faucets ran, the garage door groaned open, car engines turned over—his father's first, then his mother's five minutes later—until finally the garage door closed shut with a clang.

He rose and shuffled down the hallway, through the kitchen and out into the living room. He glanced out the window at the empty street before going back to the kitchen, the whole time feeling like a ghost haunting his own house. The silence was too complete.

He sat down at the kitchen table and dipped a spoon into his bowl of Wheaties. His father had left a note on top of the morning paper. *Jobs are in Section D. Happy Hunting. Don't sleep all day.* Nick paged through the paper, pulled out the classifieds and put them aside. He couldn't go back to accounting, but didn't know what to look for instead.

He opened the Entertainment section and spread it out on the table. He had to go all the way to the last page, in the bottom corner, where the two-inch-tall ad, with print so small he had to hunch over to read it, listed what shows were coming up at the 321.

That afternoon his phone rang and when he picked it up there was only music in the background—it sounded like the Stooges—and two women's voices. "Hello?" he said.

"Who's this?" said one of the voices.

"Victoria, it's Nick. You called me."

She chuckled. "No. Bird did. She's randomly dialing numbers in my datebook."

From behind her, Bird yelled, "I called the only guy whose last name wasn't 'Skin.'"

"I have to fix my hair," Victoria said. "Here."

"What is there left to fix?" Bird said.

"Take the phone."

Victoria must have slipped her hand over the receiver. Their voices were muffled now. Nick waited. He didn't have anything else to do.

Finally, Bird came on. "Dude." Over the phone her husky voice sounded smaller, not as forceful.

"Why do you always call me 'dude'"?

"It's what I call everybody."

"I have a name."

"No *way*. Does *everybody* have one of those?"

"You don't even remember it."

"I do. Nicholas."

"Nick."

"I hate saying that. It's like calling somebody a small scratch or a minor contusion. Like, 'hey, Paper Cut, how the hell are ya?'"

"You're one to talk."

"You're named after a mild flesh wound."

"Well, what's yours? Your real name?"

"Oh shit, would you look at the time."

"Come on."

"All my friends call me 'Bird.' But you can call me 'Bird,' too. Ha ha."

"You're hilarious."

"So. I saw you moping at the bar."

"I wasn't moping."

"Yeah, you were. Like somebody ran over your dog. How come you weren't in the pit?"

"I was . . . thinking."

"Wow. You're probably the first person in the world to do that at a Murphy's Law show. Seriously, man, I didn't think you were going to stick around."

"Why's that?"

"Between Vicky's blabbing about you, and me giving you noise, and Austin getting up in your face, I figured you'd split."

"I never considered that." This was true. Even when he'd thought he was going to get punched in the face, he'd never thought of leaving. He was surprised to realize that.

"So what were you thinking about so hard?"

"I don't know." He hesitated. What he wanted to tell her was that, last night, leaning on the bar, looking at the pit, the band, Bird and Rat dancing, even the bored bouncer slumped against the exit, he'd had an odd thought: This is what it's like to be alive. Everyone was doing exactly what they wanted to. They weren't just trudging along. He'd never seen that before. He wanted to be like that, too.

But he didn't know how to say all that to her. "I can't remember," he said.

"Bullshitter. Hey—" She coughed into the phone. "Sorry about that."

"What were you going to say?"

"Ever go to the Sunday matinees right when they open the doors? Like when they're doing sound checks?"

"No."

"It's cool. They have all the lights on but really dim so the glow doesn't reach all the way to the floor. And it's spooky quiet. Like the quiet before a bomb goes off."

"That does sounds cool."

"I dig it."

"Why are you telling me?"

"No reason."

"Are you going to be there next Sunday?"

"Maybe. I don't know. Get there early. Check it out."

"OK." Then he said, "You didn't dial me at random, did you?"

"Gotta go!" she said with a quick laugh. "Later."

Then a click as she hung up.

He put the phone down. He went to his window and looked out on the empty sunlit back yard. The lawn was turning yellow in the summer heat. So odd that Bird had called just then. He'd been thinking about her all day, and how, even after their conversations had ended, he felt like they were still talking to each other, like there was always more to say.

He wondered if she felt the same way.

One week later, he was back in the glass, high-ceilinged lobby of his old office, sitting silently in the stiff-backed metal chairs with a bunch of people he didn't recognize. Some wore suits. Maybe they had new jobs already. Others were in sweats, the men unshaven, the women with hair pulled back in ponytails. Each held the letter from the corporate headquarters in Delaware—he hadn't even known the company had a headquarters in Delaware—instructing them to come in to *finalize the transition*.

Nick had on black engineer boots, gray Hüsker Dü t-shirt, and a thick black leather belt with large metal rings dangling from it. He'd used that stuff Bird had told him about and his hair stood up in points like a pincushion. Nobody looked at him.

When the receptionist called his name, he went up the carpeted steps, pausing on the second floor where the training rooms were. Long tables were laid out in the hallway, with stacks of napkins and wire baskets full of silverware. Was there going to be a party after they gave out the last paychecks and sent them home?

On the third floor, he went to the only office with its lights on.

"Hello, Nicholas." Gary stood. He looked Nick up and down. "Well." He seemed to ponder what to say next, then decided on, "Have a seat. We'll get you out of here as quickly as we can." He leaned back in his chair and paged through papers. "We'll need you to read over and sign a few things before you leave." He slid the stacks across and held out a pen. "Just sign on any line that says 'claimant.' This is to certify the liability release. And I put X's in the areas you have to initial. To indicate you've read over the material."

Nick took the pen. He flipped through the text and signed on the first blank line. He continued, putting his small *NL* next to the areas Gary had marked. It all seemed familiar. Then he realized he was curled over Gary's desk the same way he'd curled over his own three floors below: like a monk hunched over a scroll, back bent, chin down. Signing his name on data entry card after data entry card until it was only an automatic twitch of the wrist, a mechanical gesture.

When he'd finished, Gary handed a typed list of temporary agencies across the desk and explained the job counseling options available. Nick folded the sheet and slipped it into his back pocket. Gary's desktop was spotless except for a few papers and a framed photo in one corner. In the photo a blonde, teen-aged girl in a yellow soccer uniform knelt on one knee, hands folded over a soccer ball balanced on the other. Smiling and squinting, the sun shining on her face, cheeks flushed.

Gary stopped talking and shifted stiffly, a frown curling the corners of his mouth. Nick lowered his chin and nodded as if listening intently. He wanted to tell Gary he wasn't checking out his daughter. He'd been drawn to the photo because it was the only thing in the entire office that seemed real.

"Well, Nicholas, you've amassed a good amount of experience for someone as young as yourself. That might balance out your lack of higher education. You may want to take advantage of this opportunity to re-evaluate what direction you want your career to take." He folded his hands. "Any plans yet? If you don't mind my asking."

"I don't know," Nick said. "Not this."

Gary waited for him to continue. Nick shrugged. Gary stared. Nick stared back and widened his eyes, lips pursed. Then he realized: it was the same face Bird always made. He leaned forward instead, trying to seem attentive. He and Gary seemed to be acting out some scene neither one seriously believed in. Why not talk about his daughter's soccer games instead? How were her grades in school? Assert something real. Because this company was meaningless. And the two of them became meaningless too as soon they entered the building. So why all the obedience to the place? What power did it have really? Probably Gary would be laid off at some point, too; maybe right after he handed out the last severance check. Then they'd all go someplace else, other glass-lined corporate offices, sit nervously in lobbies in suits waiting to be interviewed, and it would start all over again.

"What about you?" Nick said. "Are they going to let you go, too?"

Gary straightened, cleared his throat and shifted the papers on his desktop. Nick guessed nobody ever asked him how he was doing. "If you don't mind," he added. "I was just curious."

"Well . . ." Gary methodically moved the papers around like he was playing solitaire. "One never knows in this business. If the board of directors wanted to goose the stock price up a few points, they'd empty this entire building." He placed his palms on the desk and glanced at Nick over the top of his glasses. "I had to walk my entire staff to the door this morning." His shoulders slumped so that a hollow opened between the lapels of his suit and his chest. "Friends I've known for years. Almost a decade, in one case."

He picked up a pen and started writing on the form in front of him, as if he wouldn't allow himself to get sidetracked into an actual conversation. But all he was doing was marking tiny squiggly lines in the boxes on the form.

"That sucks," Nick said.

"Exactly." Gary nodded. "Nature of the beast, as they say."

"That doesn't make it right."

"I would've said the same thing, at your age. No offense. I don't mean to sound patronizing."

Nick shook his head. "It's OK."

Gary glanced at the photo on his desk. "As you get older, certain . . ." He searched for the word. "Concessions, if you will, come into play. In order to gain the life you want for you and your family members, compromises must be made. And you always have to prepare for contingencies. Because you never know when things like this may occur."

Nick nodded sympathetically. He couldn't detect any anger or injustice in Gary's voice, only weariness, as if this were something he'd told himself so often it too was meaningless. His face never lost its stolid, stoic expression, even looking at his daughter's picture. Maybe this was as much emotion as he was capable of, after years of maintaining the detached, professional demeanor required of him.

"No regrets, though," Gary said. "When I was younger, around your age, I never would've had the courage to do what you're doing. To join a band. Pursue your passion."

Nick burst out laughing. "I'm not in a band!"

"Oh, I'm sorry . . ." He gestured towards Nick. "The way you're dressed. I, I thought—"

"That's OK." He laughed again. "No offense taken. This is just . . ." He glanced down at himself. "This is just me." He stared at his boots. "I don't have any talent for music or anything. I wish I was good at something like that. Something besides accounting."

"Yes. Well . . . shall we get this over with?" Gary arranged the papers in a neat stack and paper-clipped them together. Then unlocked his desk drawer and pulled out an envelope. Nick's last check. Gary handed it to him. "Please tell the receptionist to send up the next person." He extended a hand. "Best of luck to you, Nicholas."

Nick rose. For some reason he couldn't fathom, he felt sad for Gary. He shook his hand firmly. "I hope you get to keep your job for a good, long time."

Gary smiled. "Thank you." He adjusted his glasses. "Thank you for saying that."

Nick stepped slowly down the stairs. It had all been very clinical. And quick. No chance of getting over to the other side of the building where his old department was. Not that he knew what he would've said to any of them. He couldn't even get angry at Gary: he wasn't the one who made the decisions here. Nobody knew who did. He stopped at the second floor. The softly-lit hallways were empty. He thought about all the newly unemployed sitting in the glass vacuum of the lobby, hands folded on their laps. He didn't care about his job, but it wasn't right that somebody—he didn't even know whose face to picture—could make a decision like that and still enjoy a catered luncheon without ever hearing one complaint, without having to see any of the consequences.

He checked the conference rooms. All empty. Even the welcome desk was abandoned. The motivational posters still lined the walls. Mountaintops and surging waterfalls and basketball players and marathon runners. *Freedom. Vision. Attitude. Your success is what comes when you pursue your dreams.* He grabbed the nearest by its frame and tried to yank it off the wall. His fingernails bent backwards.

"What the hell!"

The frame was bolted to the wall. He clenched a tight fist and punched the poster. His fist bounced off thick plastic. His knuckles scraped across the sharp edge of the frame, shredding skin. "Damn."

He paced back to the welcome desk to get a letter opener or scissors or something. Along the way he rubbed his scraped knuckles along the wall, leaving a long red streak on the cream-colored wallpaper. He yanked open the top desk drawer. Paper clips, ballpoint pens, a pack of gum, a black magic marker. He picked up the marker. *Permanent Ink. Use with Caution. Will Stain.*

Perfect.

He raced back to the hallway and went to work.

Freedom
Move to the Rhythm of Your True Spirit and You Will Set
Yourself Free **to collect unemployment**

Vision
~~The Longest Journey is the Journey Inward~~
**open your eyes and see your place in the american
waste**

Success
Your success ~~is what comes when you pursue your dreams.~~
is a cheap holiday in other people's misery

**Your "career" = a life sentence
Enjoy your meal**

Sunday evening, Nick crossed the parking lot of the 321 with long, swinging strides, the steel rings on his belt jingling, heavy boots kicking up gravel. The doors had just opened and a few people lingered around their cars, radios blasting. When a police car lumbered past, shouts echoed from one end of the lot to the other.

"The man is in the parking lot! The man is in the parking lot!"

A girl stopped in front of Nick. Skinny legs in black tights and thick-soled combat boots. Dark hair falling down over her eyes. "A dollar so I can get in? All I need's a dollar."

"Sorry," Nick said. "I only have enough for myself."

The floodlight above the wooden door was a dull halo in the growing dusk. He didn't know who was going to be inside. If Austin might go after him again. Or maybe one of the skinheads. If Bird would be there.

The alcove stank like cigarettes and something faint but sour and rank like vomit. Inside the club a band was tuning up. A dribble of bass. Abrupt rat-ta-tat of drums. Guitar feedback snaking in and out.

Someone tapping a microphone. "Check. Check one. Check."

The bouncer slouched down off his stool and scowled. "Guess you think you're a lifer now."

Nick raised his chin. "Yeah."

"See how long that lasts," he muttered. "Put your fucking hands up, ace."

Inside, the house lights were on but they were so dim the whole club looked like it was deep underwater. Motes of dust drifted overhead, stirred by the slowly revolving ceiling fans way up in the girders. Shadows darkened every corner. Bartenders lumbered back and forth, lugging bags of ice and cases of beer. The dance floor was empty. There was no music, no sound at all, except for an occasional cough and crushed ice sliding into plastic coolers.

He looked around. On the black wooden bleachers that ran along the side wall, sat Bird, elbows on knees, eyes downcast, still as a stone. He went to approach her, but stopped. She held a cigarette between thumb and index, but didn't raise it to her mouth. Instead, she stared intently at the floor, a deep frown etched on her smooth face. Motionless, as if she were balancing a great weight and any movement would tip it. He stayed where he was, afraid to interrupt.

Finally, she stirred, released a long sigh, and rubbed her forehead with the back of one hand. Then she looked over at him.

"Holy shit," he said. "Did you almost smile just now?"

"*No.*" She shook her head, eyes still distant.

"How are you?"

She took a drag on her cigarette. "Won-der-ful." She dragged out each syllable in a sarcastic drone, mimicking the Circle Jerks song.

"You sure?"

"Were you watching me?"

"Yes. Sorry. I didn't want to . . . you looked like you had a lot on your mind. Are you, uh—?"

She pointed her cigarette at him. "Don't ask." She was trying to slip into her usual swagger, but there was pleading in her voice. "OK?"

"Sure."

"OK. Come here." She got up and he followed her to the back where she and Victoria and the rest always hung out. There was no one around. She dropped beneath the bar and sat down on the footrest, then pointed at the wall. "Watch. They're testing the lights."

He sat down next to her. The stage spots flashed circles of color against the wall, red then yellow then white then red again, each one overlapping the other in a hypnotic pattern. It reminded him of blinking Christmas tree lights.

"Be better if they had more than three colors," Bird said. "But whatever. It's still cool. Gives me ideas for paintings."

He rested the back of his head against the bar. They stared at the lightshow in contented silence. He wanted to take her hand, if only to comfort her—she seemed so troubled—but somehow knew if he did, she'd never share this with him again. And he wanted to stay. With her, he didn't feel the distance, that self-doubt and awkwardness he felt with everyone else. In spite of what she'd said at the last show, with her, he might have a chance to be his real self, not the half-person he felt like at work, at home, in the rest of the world.

As roadies crossed the stage, gripping guitars by the necks or carrying drum kits over their shoulders, their silhouettes bobbed and flickered against the wall. "It's like that Plato story about the shadows in the cave," Nick said.

"Oh, yeah." A wry smile. "I was *totally* just thinking that." She leaned back, face calm now. "Anyway. Like I said, I'm here before all the Sunday shows. This is where I hang." She nodded, as if that was all he needed to know.

They met there every Sunday for the rest of the summer. Later, he would wonder what had gone wrong. Because, for him, it had been the first time he'd felt hopeful in as long as he could remember.

B SIDE

September 1987 - November 1988

Early to finish
I was late to start

—Minor Threat, "Minor Threat"

8

TOKENS & SIGNS II

Oz leaned his elbows on the bar, covered his mouth with both pudgy hands and coughed a deep, cigarette-racked cough. After talking non-stop for the last twenty minutes, his voice was going. Nick waited for him to finish.

"But you're not getting it," Oz said hoarsely. He took a sip from a plastic cup and swallowed hard. "That feeling is not unique. Sorry to break it to you. And it's not *in* you, like something innate you carry around."

"It's a symptom of society," Nick said.

"No, it's not. Stop being glib and going for the quick answers. It's not like crack or AIDs or . . . *Republicans.*" Oz laughed. "It's not inside you. Not in society. It's you *and* society—the outside world— together that causes it. Your existence in society."

He stared at Nick from behind tiny round wire-rimmed glasses. He had dark, timid eyes and bloated round cheeks that crowded a small mouth. "And once you're aware of this—this 'gap,' let's call it—you never lose it." He tapped one side of his head with an index finger. "It's always up here. And once you're aware of how ridiculous and absurd everything is, you can't go back. You can't be retroactively ignorant."

"But you can change."

"Really? How?"

Nick paused. "You can remove yourself from the world."

"You can't choose not to exist. Even throwing yourself in front of a train won't change anything. You exist whether you want to or not. And mere existence is a bending. You know what that's from?" He squinted at Nick.

He hesitated, not sure how to pronounce the name. "Sartre . . ?"

"Right."

"By existing, you're in the way."

"You can't help but be." Oz nodded. "But the trick is, how do you keep from getting run over? How do you maintain your, your . . ." He thumped at his heart with one fist. "Without being consumed by the whole tidal wave of bullshit."

"But bending means you're going to be shaped by all the bullshit," Nick said.

"To a point. But it doesn't define you. You see what I'm saying? We're not exclusively a product of all the bullshit around us and we're not de facto what we *are*, either . . ."

Bird squeezed in between them and leaned on the bar. Crow waited right behind her. Oz leaned to talk around them. ". . . we make ourselves what we are."

"Jesus Christ." Bird snickered. "They're still talking."

Crow nodded toward Nick. "I liked him more when he was quiet and bumbling."

"Yeah, now he's just bumbling," Bird said.

"No luck getting into the back bar?" Nick said.

Bird shook her head. "The guy we thought was a new guy was just the same old guy with a new haircut."

"Guy's a dipshit," Crow said. "I didn't even get to try out my fake ID." She held up a driver's license. "Check this out. I'm officially twenty-three years old."

"Happy birthday."

"Doesn't it look real? We're trying to scrape money together for beer. Austin's parents are away so we're rounding everybody up. So far, it's me, Rat, Austin and some of the north Jersey crew."

"What about Bird?"

"She's not hanging after. So, got any money?"

He had thirty-two dollars in his pocket, but that was all until his next temp job came through. He'd spent his severance on the shows at the 321. And on albums, and groceries for his parents so he wouldn't feel like a complete freeloader. "I don't really have any cash." He had no idea when the next temp job would come through.

"Whatever." Crow tapped Bird on the shoulder. "Hey, bitch. I'm gonna go scrounge outside."

"Later, slut."

Nick said to Bird, "So what happened last Sunday?"

They'd been meeting here for two months now, before everyone else showed up, but she hadn't been at last Sunday's show. Nick had stood fidgeting and shuffling his feet at the bar, until Oz called him over. "So, our little friend has flown the coop, eh?" he'd said.

Now Bird didn't seem to hear him. He leaned over to ask again but she glanced over his shoulder and shouted, "Hey, Sid!"

Austin came clumping over in his oversized combat boots. "Don't call me that!" He cast a sideways glance at Nick, head bowed. "What's going on?"

Nick stiffened.

"Don't sweat, dude," Austin said. "Victoria dumped me a while ago."

"Surprise, surprise," Bird said.

"She's with some guy in the Crew," Austin said. "Think they're gonna come after me now?"

Oz motioned to the entrance on the other side of the bar. "You could ask them."

A group of skinheads, shirtless, wearing jeans with red suspenders, came out of the dark hallway that led into the club. Victoria walked with them, head held high as if they were her palace escort. But none of them were paying any attention to her, except for a tall lean one who had a hand on her back. Her head was shaved bald, with one lone blonde braid dangling over her left eye. Her gaze searched the bar, locking for a second on Bird's face, then Nick's, before glancing away.

Bird lit her cigarette with a quick flick of a pink Bic lighter. Nick turned to her. She had been watching him watching Victoria. Austin backed into the nearest wall and folded his arms, eyes on the Crew as they moved towards the stage.

"Watch my seat," Oz told Bird. "I'm going over to the dark side." He lumbered down off his stool. "Otherwise known as the men's room."

"Bombs away," Bird said. She took a long drag on her Newport, then squinted at Nick through the gray haze, smoking like an old-time movie star, like Bette Davis, elbow resting on one hip, palm up, wrist bent back, cigarette between two fingers.

"What?" he said.

"You know."

"I'm not like her. In spite of what you think."

Bird took a sip from her soda, then put the cup down and stared at the bubbles slowly rising. Without her friends around, she was always quiet and thoughtful. But tonight she seemed hesitant. It was strange.

"Yeah, maybe. You're different now."

"I'm glad you finally noticed," he said. "Only took two months, huh?"

"So you've been actually, like, counting the days?"

He rested his elbows on the bar. "So where've you been? I tried calling."

She winced and looked around the bar.

"OK," Nick said. "Sorry I asked."

"My folks don't give me messages," she said. "They're kind of defective that way."

"You missed Adrenaline OD."

"I know."

"I thought you liked them."

"Yeah." She shrugged. "I dig them, on occasion." She stared down at her cigarette, lips pursed.

Nick had no idea what he'd suddenly said wrong. A Hüsker Dü song came on over the PA. "The Girl Who Lives on Heaven Hill." The guitar sounded like wind whipping through a long tunnel. The singer's voice was strained and desperate.

Bird looked over one shoulder. "Hey, Sidney. You don't have to hide. Nobody comes back here."

Austin glared at her, then came over and sat down on the next stool. "I'm not hiding."

She turned to Nick, her back to Austin. "See how quiet he is with me?"

"Yeah," Nick said. "Very docile. Why is that?"

"We went to school together. I knew him when he was a preppy.

On the soccer team and everything. Baggy shorts and alligator shirts. All that silly shit."

He glanced over at Austin. "What changed?"

Bird shrugged. "Heard the right song on the radio, I guess." She turned back to Austin. "That's Oz's seat."

"So?"

"Whatever." Bird scowled. "Be a hardass."

Austin sneered. "That guy weirds me out."

"He's OK," Nick said.

"He's a freaking chickenhawk."

"I have no idea what that is."

"A fag scrounging for high schoolers. He sits around waiting to hook up."

"You're kidding." Nick glanced at Bird but she only shrugged. "Well, so what?"

"It's fucking gross," Austin said. "The guy's like thirty and he's checking out all these like tenth graders or something."

"No," Nick said. "He's not. He sits there every show and reads a book. He hardly talks to anybody except me and Bird."

"I never said he *got* to hook up with any tenth grader, dude. Nobody'll go near him. But that's what he *wants* to do. Why does he sit here drinking sodas when he's old enough to get real drinks in the back?"

"I don't believe it."

"Ask Bird."

"How would I know?" she said.

"We were just talking about books," Nick said. "He didn't do anything."

"I don't know, man," Austin said. "How come he never leaves this spot? It's like he's camping out here. It's weird."

Bird wiggled her fingers in the air. "Whooooohh, it's crrreepy," she said, rolling her R's.

"And there's something about the way he talks. It's odd."

"Yeah," Bird said. "He uses, like, actual *words.*"

Austin snorted. "You know what I mean."

"You're a dipshit." Bird turned to face him. "He sits back here because he got his ass kicked by the Crew. He knows they won't ratpack anybody at the bar."

"No way," Austin said. "For real? Did they go after him because he likes boys?"

"No," Bird said. "They went after him because they're assholes. Just like you."

Oz came weaving his way to the back of the bar.

"I'm gonna ask him," Austin said.

"What the hell?" Nick said. "Leave him alone."

He'd seen so many fights here in the last few months. Always over something stupid—the wrong kind of haircut, a dirty look—and always unbalanced. Several guys surrounding one guy, pulling him down by the collar and jumping on him. The image of Oz caught up in something like that made his stomach tighten.

"What's up?" Oz said.

Nobody spoke. Oz looked around, puzzled. Nick tried to think of something else to talk about.

"What?" Oz raised an eyebrow.

Bird leaned into Austin. "Don't be a dick, Sidney."

He shrugged her off. "Bird said you got messed up by the Crew?"

"Oh, that." Oz wiped his palms on the front of his flannel shirt. "Not the Crew. It was some other gaggle of boy scouts out of Philadelphia."

"I was there," Bird said. "They had to peel him off the floor."

"Well, consider it." Oz gestured with both hands like he was conducting a lecture. "Standing upright, I was exposed on all sides. By lying face down, I removed half the potential targets on my body."

"Yeah," Bird said. "And they all tripped over each other trying to kick him in the ribs. Then they tried to drag him around but he wrapped his arms around one of the skinhead's legs so they couldn't move him."

Oz pulled a cigarette from the pack in his chest pocket. "I assumed all nobility was lost at that point."

"And the big skin's screaming, 'Get this loser off me! Get him off me!' Then the bouncers came in and tossed them all out."

"You should've at least tried to get some shots in," Austin said.

"My friend," Oz said. "You can't beat them that way."

"How would you know? You didn't try."

"They always win," Oz said. "But they never last. A closed system cannot sustain itself."

Austin stared. "I have no fucking clue what you just said."

Oz sighed. "My friend, the only way to win is to outlast your enemy."

Austin glanced at Nick, a slight leer playing across his face, then said to Oz, "OK. But why'd they go after you in the first place, man?"

Oz blinked at Austin a few times. "They need a reason?"

"I was just asking, dude."

"And I'm asking you. What possible reason could they have?"

Austin shrugged. "I don't know. I'm not them."

"Because there is no reason to it," Oz said quietly.

"Yeah. Maybe."

"That's the whole point."

"Yeah. Maybe that's it."

"No," Oz said. "That is it entirely. There is no reason. If you think there is, then you're one of them. Reason takes thought, and that's something they're not capable of. And tell me, what possible justification is there for eight grown men to jump one defenseless man?"

Austin leaned forward, bobbing his knees up and down. Oz stood very still, eyes fixed on him.

"Don't give the fascists that much credit," Oz said finally.

Austin nodded solemnly. He seemed humbled. "All right, Oz. I didn't mean anything. Just asking." He stood and waved a hand towards the empty stool. "Here."

Oz sat down without a word. He motioned to the bartender for another soda, then stared out at the empty stage, shoulders slouched, unlit cigarette pinched between his fingers. Bird took out her lighter, flicked it and held the flame out. He didn't seem to notice.

"Fire here, Oz."

"Oh." He blinked. "Forget it. I don't even know why I took this out."

"Here she comes," Austin said. "I'm going up front."

Victoria wound her way around the bar, a tall, lean skinhead close behind. "Hey," she said. "This is Mike Skin. Mike, that's Austin who just left. That's Bird. That's Oz back there not paying attention. And that's Nick."

"I seen you before." Mike Skin nodded. "In the pit."

"He likes to thrash," Victoria said.

"I know. I seen you." He nodded approval, then put a hand on Victoria's back. "Catch you later," he said and walked off.

With a glance toward Mike, Bird whispered in Nick's ear, "They can't last long in the wild, separated from the pack."

Crow came up behind Victoria and wrapped her arms around her. "'Take the skinheads bowling,'" she sang. "'Take them bowling . . .'"

Victoria giggled. "You just missed Mike."

Crow looked around. "Where'd they go? I want to meet some."

"Ew." Bird wrinkled her nose. "Crow."

"What? Some of them are cute."

"They're jock assholes pretending to be hardcore."

"Jocks have nice muscles."

Bird rolled her eyes. "Way to support the scene, sister."

"Later days, losers," Crow said, walking away with a languid wave.

"Stay away from Mike!" Victoria called after her. She held out a handful of black shoelaces to Bird. "Do you have any room left in one of your pockets?"

Bird took the laces and glanced at Victoria's feet. "What's holding your boots on?"

Victoria lifted her skirt. Her combat boots were laced up to the top with black and white shoelaces. "Mike gave these to me," she said. "It means I'm skin."

Bird clapped her hands in mock joy. "Oh boy, I'm so happy for you, honey! When's the wedding? When you gonna start popping out little skinhead babies?"

Nick said, "Actually, most babies *are* skinheads, when you think about it."

"I bet they'll even have little steel-toed combat booties," Bird said.

"Mike's cool, Bird," Victoria said, her soft voice almost lost in their laughter. "I love him."

"You love everybody." Bird shrugged. "That's the problem." She pointed at Nick. "It's weird to see Prettyboy laugh."

"I'm so glad you two can amuse each other," Victoria said.

Bird wrapped her arms around Victoria and pressed her face against her shoulder. "Just playing, Vic."

"I know."

Bird reached up and tugged her braid. "So, what's up? You gonna be the first bald super model?"

"I bought some wigs. I love them, Bird. I can be anybody I want with a wig." She cast a sideways glance at Nick. "Stop staring at my head."

"I can't help it," he said. "You look so different."

She turned to Bird. "Does it look bad?"

Nick said, "I tried to picture it when you told me over the phone, but still. It's a big change."

"You have no hair, Vicky," Bird said. "What do you want me to say?"

"But do I look awful?"

Nick and Bird both tilted their heads and considered her face. Beneath the smooth, gleaming dome of her scalp, the braid dangling like a comma on her forehead, her pale eyes seemed larger, her small mouth even smaller. There was nothing to hide her sad gaze. Her face stood out now like a dare. She looked from Nick to Bird and back. "You guys are making me nervous."

"No," Nick said. "I like it."

"Me too. You should've done it a long time ago, Vic."

"Thanks." She smiled a wide smile, happy creases in the corner of her eyes.

Over the PA, the DJ droned, "7 Seconds up in a few minutes, folks. Do I need to go over this again? No stagediving. No chickenfights. No walls of death. And absolutely, under any circumstances, no vogueing."

"Let's go up front," Victoria said. She turned to go, then shouted over one shoulder to Bird. "Don't leave without me. I forgot my keys."

"You're staying with her?" Nick said.

"Yeah."

"Like visiting?"

"No." She hesitated. It was the first time he'd seen her look unsure. "I moved into her place. That's where I was last week. Moving."

"What?" He couldn't tell if she was kidding or not.

"Yeah. I'm down in Philly now."

"I didn't know you were moving."

"I had to get out of my house. Vicky said she'd take care of my half of the rent until I got myself set up."

"I had no idea," he said.

She shrugged. She seemed stunned by his reaction. "Don't look like I ran over your dog."

"Are you doing that same thing's she doing?" Nick said. "The modeling?"

She winced. "Right. 'Modeling.' No way. I'll find a part-time gig at a Kinko's or something like that. Some place with a copier so I can sneak in my zines."

He rubbed his chin. Why did everything always race past him?

"I was going to tell you."

"So," he said. "How often are you going to come up here, then?"

"Not much, I guess. Not with Vic's shit car. And I can't borrow my parents' car up in Collingswood, obviously." After a while, she added, "We'll still come here sometimes. It's not like it's *that* far away or anything. And there's decent clubs down there."

He nodded. "I know."

"No big deal, right?"

"I know."

"You got a car. You can come down."

"I know." He shook his head, still confused. "Why didn't you tell me?"

Bird cocked her head back and blew a cloud of smoke upward in a long sigh. "I'm telling you now." She shrugged.

"I don't understand." He faltered. "I thought, I thought you liked hanging here. With me, I mean."

The house lights went down and the crowd in front of the stage cheered. He slumped against the bar. His head felt heavy. Every Sunday evening this summer, he'd waited at the back of the bar, watching for Bird to weave past the massive bouncers, chin up, eyes searching the crowd for him. And every time she'd shown up. Waiting for her, watching the dark hallway, he'd felt an unfamiliar certainty. Confidence, even. But now he just felt stupid. Again.

He had thought this was leading somewhere, that maybe eventually they could be together. A misguided hope, he guessed. She'd never replied to any of his hints to meet someplace else beside the 321. And all the time they'd spent sitting beside each other, they'd never touched. But the few times he would place his hand on her back, or lean close to confide something, she hadn't pulled away, either. Maybe he should've been more direct. But it was Bird. That wouldn't have worked. Too late now anyway.

She bowed her head. "Don't be so bummed," she said quietly.

He turned to leave, then stopped himself. "You coming?"

"Hold on. Wait." She dug around in the pockets of her jacket and pulled out a cassette tape. "Here. Take this."

"What is it?"

"A mix tape. Not much of a mix though. All Dead Milkmen songs I got off the radio."

"You made me a tape?"

"No. It's mine. I didn't finish with it yet. But you can have it."

"Why are you giving it to me?"

She shrugged.

"You're going to disappear, aren't you?"

As soon as he said it, he recalled Victoria, staring down at him as he sat in his car waiting to pull away. This must've been how she felt: afraid to want someone but unable to stop.

"Dude. Take the tape."

"OK," he said. "Thanks."

"If you haven't figured it out yet . . ." She took a last drag on the cigarette and pinched it between thumb and forefinger. "I'm kind of a messed-up person. You don't want to get to know me."

"But I do know you."

She slowly shook her head.

"Well, I at least know you're not a messed-up person."

"Listen to you. All confident and shit." She smiled weakly.

He tucked the tape into his field jacket. "Well. Thanks." He looked down at the pins on the front of the jacket and pulled one off. "Here."

She squinted at it.

"It's Franz Kafka."

"Oh, joy. I have, like, all his albums."

Applause came up from the crowd. 7 Seconds had come on and were plugging in guitars. The lead singer wore a bandanna and baggy shorts. His name was Kevin Seconds. He had black greasepaint under his eyes like a football player. "Hello!" he shouted cheerfully into the microphone. "Trenton skins, all right." The crowd whistled and clapped.

Bird took one last drag. The bartenders leaned on the cash registers, arms folded, eyes on the stage.

"You know when you said I was different now?" Nick said.

"Yeah?" She looked up at him but still seemed far away.

"I'm different because of you."

She stared down at her cigarette.

Victoria came back to the bar, silhouetted by the lights from the stage. "Let's go, you guys."

"All right," Nick said.

"The pit is huge." Victoria turned away and headed for the crowd.

"Bird," Nick said. "You coming?"

From the stage, Kevin Seconds yelled, "Here goes!"

Bird flicked the cigarette with a snap of her fingers. It bounced against the wall in a burst of orange sparks. She stepped into him, head cast back, round face smooth and white in the glare from the stage lights, dark eyes hard and glistening. He pulled her toward him, his lips parted.

"No," she said. "Closed."

He closed his mouth. She lifted her arms and held his face between her palms. Her hands were warm. She pressed her lips to his, softly and quickly. It felt like a memory even as it was happening.

The music stopped. Feedback quivered in the air. The band hunched over their guitars, mouths hanging open. Sweat dripped off their chins. People in the pit were bent over, hands on knees, sides heaving. A young guy shoved his way out of the crowd, a fist clamped over his nose, blood pouring between his fingers. Two bouncers dragged a skinny mohawked boy to the side doors. One had the kid's right arm twisted behind his back. The kid sneered, raising a middle finger as he was jerked across the floor. The bouncers kicked the side doors open and a warm breeze drifted in. Outside, rain was falling in silver streaks beneath the floodlight. Shiny black puddles dotted the lot. The bouncers pushed the kid outside, then slammed the doors with a bang.

The band picked out a few random notes. "Be cool," Kevin

Seconds said. He couldn't stop pacing across the stage. "We're all in this together."

Austin wrapped one arm around Nick's shoulders.

"What the hell," Nick said.

"Wall of death."

Austin's face was shiny and flushed red. With his other arm, he grabbed the guy next to him around the shoulders. The crowd shifted, pressing close together. Fingers grabbed Nick's sleeve and pulled him backwards. He heard Bird shouting behind him. "Go back more!"

The entire pit pushed back in a wall of linked arms. The dance floor slowly opened up. Dirty bootprints covered the black and white checkerboard. The wall pushed back further, then stopped, forming a half circle facing the stage. The band watched curiously, hands at their sides. The bassist shrugged, adjusted his guitar strap and pounded out the pulsing opening of "We're Gonna Fight."

Two bouncers ran up to the wall and pulled at people's shirts, but everyone hung onto to each other, fingers clutching sleeves or hooked into belts.

"Play the song!" somebody shouted.

The bassist repeated the same thudding notes while the rest of the band stared down at the wall of people. Kevin Seconds looked back at the drummer. The drummer counted off. A sullen roar of guitar ripped out of the speakers. Kevin leapt up, back arched, then landed with knees bent, crouched over the microphone. *We're gonna fight! We know who's right!"*

Bird's tiny fists beat against Nick's back. "Go! Fucking go!"

The wall charged full speed, leaping up at the last second and cresting like a wave at the front of the stage. Bodies flipped end over end, arms flailing. The bouncers kneeling at the side of the stage rushed out and started hurling people back into the crowd. The kid in front of Nick—ragged shirt, long stringy sweat-soaked hair—tripped and Nick landed with a grunt on his back, all the air slammed from his lungs. Hands gripped his belt, his jacket, the back of his neck, and yanked him up and off his feet. The lights on the ceiling wheeled past. Still held aloft, he skidded across upraised hands and rolled over, face down. Hands pressed against his chest, stomach and hips, propelling him forward. Austin leapt off the stage and plummeted past in a blur.

Nick reached out, fingers inches from the plywood railing of the stage. He saw the confusion of black cables duct-taped to the scratched floorboards, Kevin Second's scuffed black and white Keds, a gash in one knee, blood trickling down his shin. Nick arched back, twisting around to look up. Kevin sang, sweat streaming down his face. He nodded at Nick like that was exactly where he should be and Nick thought *yeah fuck yeah fuck my stupid job fuck my parents fuck Victoria fuck Bird fuck everybody this is the only thing that makes sense* and when Kevin leaned over and put the mike in Nick's face he screamed *"YEEAAAAAHHHH!"* so loud his voice cracked and hands lifted him up and he pressed his palms into the dirt and sawdust of the stage and strained to pull himself up over the railing.

A bouncer's broad palm closed over his face. "Not tonight, asshole."

With a flick of his wrist, he sent Nick tumbling back into the crowd.

9

OUT OF STEP

The Sunrise Diner on Friday afternoon was cool and bright. One long window filled the front wall and looked out over the parking lot and the continuous traffic on Route One. Mirrors lined the other three walls, so wherever they turned they saw one anothers' reflections: Nick, Crow, Rat and Austin. The tables around them were empty. In a far corner sat two men and a woman—all in suits—frowning over paperwork as they poked at salads. An old couple sat by the window, laughing with the young waitress. Nick and the others gazed around in silence. They came here a lot, but the waitresses never acknowledged them beyond taking their orders, much less laughed or joked. And the tall, stooped, balding man at the front rolled his eyes whenever they came through the door and made them wait for a table even when the place was empty.

"I don't know where Victoria and Bird are," Rat said. "Should I call them again?"

"No," Crow said. "They're not going to come all the way up here just to sit in a lame-ass diner."

"I wasn't asking you," Rat said quietly. She bent over her menu, downcast and pouting, chubby forearms crossed. Her green and yellow hair was pulled up in wavering plumes the way Victoria had used to do hers. Crow had laughed when she'd seen it and said, "Just because Vic isn't around anymore doesn't mean you can be her now."

Nick said, "You think they'll come to the Cro-Mags show?"

"Victoria might, cause Mike Skin'll be there," Rat said.

"Not me," Crow said. "Those skins think they're so hard. I tried talking to them last time." She smirked. "They try to cover it up, but they're like ten years old. They still think girls are icky."

"I want to go," Nick said.

Crow snickered. "It's so funny you're into such a dumb-ass hardcore band."

"That's what's cool about them."

The Cro-Mags didn't have the speed and zeal of 7 Seconds or the range of Hüsker Dü. They were what they were—a solid hardcore band—and that was all they could do. Nick admired the simplicity and honesty.

"I'm going," Austin said. "The pit'll be fierce."

Crow flipped the laminated pages of the oversized menu. "I want something good for once. I'm starving." She had let her hair down to hang straight past her chin, framing her narrow face. "Prettyboy, buy me something."

"No."

"Come on. You have money."

"*Had* money. No job now."

"You just said you were working."

"That was a temp job. It was only for two days."

"They fired you after two days?"

"'Temp' means temporary, Crow."

She closed the menu. "Guess it's cheese fries and chicken strips again."

Nick looked at the people in suits, then at the old couple. You could always tell the difference between people who had to be somewhere and the ones who could take their time. He still hadn't learned how to do that. He felt like he was on a vacation he hadn't earned.

"You gotta get out of that shit, man," Austin said. "Try some new kind of job."

He'd thought about it, but he was only good at accounting. He was trying to accept that. Because at least he had this one boring skill. Otherwise, he'd be drifting, perpetually broke, like Victoria and the rest. He shrugged. "Guess I like having a paycheck too much."

"Filthy yuppie scum," Crow said, absently poking her straw at the ice cubes in her glass of water.

"Well, what do you guys want to do? For a job, I mean."

"Like, what are my 'career goals'?" Crow snorted. "How *old* are you, Prettyboy?"

"Nineteen. Only about a year older than you."

Rat shrugged. "I'm not good at anything."

"That can't be true," Nick said. "What do you like to do?"

"I like to draw."

"You can't turn anything you like into a job," Crow said. "You don't like what you do but you do it anyway."

Austin drummed on the table. "I'm not doing what my old man does. That's for damn sure."

"What does he do?" Nick said.

"I don't know. He wears a suit."

"Oh yeah," Crow said. "I've seen that guy. He's in the window at Macy's."

"Your dad's a mannequin?" Rat giggled. "That's so sad."

"He's always pissed off," Austin told Nick. "Comes home late and falls asleep on the couch. With his fucking suit still on. That's his career. That's his whole fucking life."

"I think that's everybody's dad," Crow said.

Austin scooted his chair around so he could see out the window, then slouched down with a lazy exhale, stretching his legs into the aisle. Usually he wore the same pair of eight-hole Doc Martens, the black leather cracked and weathered in a way Nick could never get his boots to look, even after he'd dug his toes into the gravel to scuff them up. But today he wore what looked like a uniform: black sneakers, black baggy pants and a plain white t-shirt. "This is what you should do with your future, dude." He pulled a flyer out of his back pocket. "They're gonna play the 321."

Nick looked at the flyer. Around a cartoon drawing of a kid in baggy pants and combat boots were scrawled the names of about ten different bands he'd never heard of.

"They're like, about something." Austin said. "None of that rock and roll bullshit."

Across the bottom, in big block letters: *I CAN'T CHANGE THE WORLD BUT I CAN CHANGE THE WORLD IN ME.*

"Austin's got the straight edge," Crow said in a sarcastic drawl.

"Really?"

Nick knew the Minor Threat song, about swearing off drinking, drugs, smoking, all to keep your head clear, maintain your edge. Growing up listening to nothing but rock stations, when every song seemed like a veiled reference to getting wasted, Nick liked that a singer had sung so fiercely about denying all that and thinking for yourself.

"It's about not deluding yourself by getting fucked up all the time," Austin said, knees bobbing. "There's like a whole army of straight edge kids. They reject all that bullshit. Keep their heads straight, you know? So nothing can throw them off."

Crow rolled her eyes. "No. They drink Yoo-hoo and roll around on skateboards."

"It's about will power." Austin pressed an index finger to his temple, staring at Nick intently. "You control yourself so nobody can control you. Know what I mean?"

"Sure." Nick nodded. He thought about all the time he spent at home now, with no job to go to, and how the days could pass by like sleep. *But I can change the world in me.* "I like that. It's philosophy in action. A way of willing yourself."

He could tell Austin didn't believe him, but he envied that clarity. His certainty in something he'd heard about maybe only a few months ago.

Austin scowled and glanced around, as if embarrassed for revealing too much. "Yeah, well." He jammed the flyer into his back pocket. "Whatever. Better than turning into a skinhead."

On the way to their cars they ended up behind the businesspeople. The woman fumbled with her purse and a file folder of papers as she walked. A plastic badge slipped out and fell on the pavement behind her.

"Hold up," Nick said.

He bent and picked it up. He recognized the logo immediately: blue slanted letters on a white background. A photo ID badge for ADR, the corporate office where he used to work. *Elizabeth Sikorsky.* Awkward smile, gray suit, stiff page-boy haircut.

The woman turned back. Nick handed her the badge. "ADR. I used to work there."

She snatched it out of his palm and spun on one high heel, shoes tapping a quick, sharp rhythm as she marched away. The fear on her face made him laugh aloud. The men stood by their car, looking concerned, but not making a move.

"What the hell," Nick said.

Crow gripped his shoulder and turned him so that he faced his reflection in a car window. Late nights had made his eye sockets hollow, the eyes themselves lost in shadow. His hair stood up in short, sharp bolts, pale scalp showing through. Round drops of dried blood dotted his Black Flag t-shirt from the bloody nose he'd gotten at the Shock Mommies show.

"Look, sweetie," Crow said, eyebrows raised. "Recognize this guy?"

Nick followed Rat's car as she slowed through the recurring stop signs, navigating the winding, wooded side streets of her development. Austin slouched in the passenger seat, arm dangling out the window. Crow sat in the back seat, popping her gum and humming "Moon over Marin."

A tape was sticking out of the cassette deck. Austin popped it in with a lazy jab. After a while, he said, "What is this shit?"

"The Dead Milkmen," Nick said.

Out of the corner of one eye, he saw Austin shaking his head. The music wasn't hardcore. All jangling guitars and nervous rhythms, songs about Camaros and laundromats and fish filets. The singer didn't sing but spoke the lyrics in a sarcastic nasal whine. The band seemed to be barely trying, and at first Nick couldn't figure out why Bird would fill almost an entire tape with their songs. *Little bit of sole and I'm feeling fine.* But after a while he recognized something defiant in the lyrics' silliness. *Little bit of sole and I'm losing my mind.* A denial of reality.

"Sounds like you recorded this in a toilet," Austin said. "It's all distorted."

"It's Bird's."

Austin was quiet for a while. The next song started, then cut out abruptly. Bird must have gotten interrupted while making the tape. There was only silence for the rest of that side. Whenever he would listen to the tape by himself, he'd let the silence play out and listen to the whisper of static.

"It's over, right?" Austin said.

When Nick nodded, he popped the tape out and tuned the radio to WTSR. "Bird's taste in music is all over the fucking place. She used to be into the Talking Heads and Devo and that new wave shit before she went hardcore."

Kids on roller skates were playing hockey in the middle of the street. Nick slowed behind Rat's car as the group sidled out of the way.

He said, "You guys went to school together, right?"

"Yeah. She was goth in high school though. Like, not a total vampire but kind of, I don't know, goth-like. Black clothes all the time, but no crazy makeup. Real quiet. She'd stare at everybody like she was gonna knife them or something. And she used to carry these notebooks with weird-ass drawings in them. Some girls took one once, tore out the pages and passed them around. She didn't carry any around after that."

"Dipshits." Nick shook his head.

"Then these prep guys used to give her shit because she was small and weird and always by herself. It was stupid."

"What guys?"

"I don't know." He shifted in his seat. "Like, just the jocks and shit." He bounced his fist against the door frame. "She was hard, though. You couldn't tell it was getting to her."

"Who were these guys?"

Austin shrugged. "The preps."

Nick glanced over at him. "This was your crew that was picking on her, wasn't it?"

"Yeah," he said with a sigh. "But I wasn't as bad as some of the other guys."

Nick frowned. "Every time I start to think you actually have some sort of redeeming trait—"

"I turn out to be an asshole." He threw up his hands. "I know I am! But I don't hang with those dickheads anymore. And once I got to know her I was the one that made them back off. Kicked the shit out of the biggest and that was the end of it. And we're cool now. Right?" He looked at Nick. "You talked to her. She's all right with me?"

He nodded. "She never said anything bad about you, if that's what you mean."

In a low drone, the DJ read off the list of shows coming up at the 321.

Austin gnawed on a thumbnail, brow furrowed. "That's cool," he said quietly.

"What's going on?" Crow said from the backseat. "I can't hear you guys."

Nick looked in the rear-view. "Austin's a stupid asshole."

"Oh. No argument here."

A squall of feedback out of his car speakers, then the quick angry chords of "Police Story." Austin reached over and turned up the volume. Rollin's screams were almost lost in the snarl of guitars. Crow sang along under her breath.

As the song came to an end, Nick said, "I can understand Victoria wanting to move out. But why did Bird go with her?"

"I don't know, man." Austin shrugged. "Bird's house freaked her out. She said it was haunted or something. Victoria thinks everything's haunted, but you know what I mean. She said it was, like, dead quiet all the time. And her folks never talked unless it was to tell her when she fucked up something, like putting the forks in the wrong drawer or some shit like that. But most of the time, they acted like she wasn't there. Maybe that was it."

"Ready to Explode" by DOA came on: a few squealing high notes, followed by a quick march of drums and guitars. The band had just played the 321.

Crow shouted, "Turn it up!"

Austin sighed and spun the volume knob.

"What's Bird's real name?" Nick asked.

"It's, uh . . ." Austin frowned. He always did when he had to think. "I can't remember. Starts with an M, I think." He laughed. "That's fucked up. Everybody's been calling her Bird for so long I can't remember her real name."

Crow said, "Why are you laughing? What're you guys saying about me?"

"Nothing," Austin said.

"We're talking about Bird," Nick shouted to her.

"I can't believe that little psycho left me alone with you losers," Crow shouted over the car seat. "Prettyboy, tell her to move back here. She listens to you."

"Why do you say that?"

"You two were hanging before the shows all the time. Never seen her talk to somebody for that long without getting bored and lighting their shoelaces on fire."

"Apparently, it didn't mean a thing," Nick muttered. The bitterness in his voice startled him.

"Still can't hear you."

"I said . . . I don't think she ever really listened to me."

"You're probably right. She doesn't listen to anybody."

"Why is that?" Nick glanced in the rear-view. "Why is she that way?"

"Seriously?" Crow thought for a moment. She blew a bubble, then popped it. He waited, hoping for an answer. She stared out the window. "Who knows with that kid."

The next week, he snagged a temp job at a small office filing stacks and stacks of computer printouts. At lunchtime, he brought his tuna fish sandwich and can of Coke to his car and drove along the wooded, narrow back roads that wound through the suburbs behind the company's building. He popped in Bird's tape, took a bite of sandwich, then laid it on his lap. He rolled down the windows. As he passed through the shade of the trees sunlight blinked on his windshield. Only forty minutes for lunch. Soon, he'd be back to four more hours standing over file drawers, but he pushed that out of his mind and settled back in his seat.

The first song sounded odd. The beat too slow, the singer's voice too deep. Nick pressed the fast forward button and released it. No sound came out of the speakers. He pressed it again. Then the rewind, steering with one hand along the narrow curving road. Nothing. He tried to find a spot to pull over, but it was all trees and hedges. Weeds sprouted out of drainage ditches on either side. He popped out the cassette to examine it, but when he pulled on it the black tape snagged on something inside the player and unspooled to flutter in the breeze blowing through the open windows.

"What the hell!" The depth of his anger took him by surprise.

Still no place to pull over. He weaved down the narrow road, one hand on the wheel, the tape in the other. He tried to keep his hand steady; every time he jerked the wheel another few inches unraveled. "Shit!"

A car sped past in a blur, honking.

"Sorry! Sorry!" he yelled, stupidly.

Finally, he pulled into somebody's driveway, took a deep breath and gingerly tried to work the narrow, black ribbon free from the slot with his fingers. If he could get it out he could use a pen to turn the wheels and spool it back inside the cassette. He tugged again, gently, and the thin acetate split in half. "Motherfucker." He threw the cassette down on the passenger seat. He made a sloppy u-turn and drove back to the office in silence. He wasn't going to turn on the radio. Too early for the college stations and he couldn't even listen to Top 40 anymore. He could no longer tell the DJs' patter apart from the commercials, the commercials from the hollow, bouncy songs they played. He made a left, then another at the next stop sign. He hadn't seen Bird since the 7 Seconds show three months ago.

It was just a mix tape, he told himself. An unfinished one, at that. But still, it was the only thing she'd ever given him.

He picked up the tape and flung it out the window.

That Sunday evening, Crow, Nick and Rat stood outside the pit, in the open space between the stage and the bar, watching Token Entry, five red-faced teenagers with shaved heads and baggy white t-shirts.

Crow eyed the crowd. "These straight edge boys are so boring."

The band was halfway through their set and had not let up at all. The pit was a blur that only stopped to shout out the choruses. Every song sounded the same, but watching the way the band thrashed and leapt around the stage, Nick wished he could be part of it. Feel whatever had taken them over.

"But they're quite violent," Crow said. "Have to give them that."

A shirtless skinhead, one of Mike Skin's crew, walked past, cackling bitterly to himself.

"What's so funny?" Nick said to Crow.

"No idea." She chewed her gum quickly, jawbone tensing and flexing in her lean face. "But something's different."

He watched the band. She was right. Something was off. Maybe the crowd. He was having a hard time telling people apart. Everybody looked the same. He shifted his feet. Maybe he just needed to move around. "I'm going in," he said.

Crow grinned. "That should be amusing."

After only a few songs a barrage of shoulders and elbows struck Nick from behind and he flipped end over end, feet flying up in the air. The back of his skull bounced against the floor.

Austin yanked him to his feet. "Dude! What the fuck!"

It sounded like someone screaming down a long tunnel. Nick blinked and shook his head.

"Stop turning around!" Austin shouted. "How the fuck can you see if you keep turning around."

He nodded. When he moved his head it felt like his brain was sloshing from one side to the other.

Austin frowned. "You all right?"

"Yeah."

Austin turned his back to Nick and faced the pit, arms out to shield him. The guys on either side pressed closer, forming a wall around him.

"I'm all right." Nick nodded again, embarrassed.

Over one shoulder, Austin yelled, "What's with you, man? Keep your fucking head up."

He nodded again. The back of his head was pulsing. It was the third time he'd been knocked down. He couldn't stop looking over at the bar. He thought he'd seen the flash of yellow hair, the quick bouncing stride.

He staggered back to Crow and Rat.

"Don't bother," Crow said to him with a sympathetic smirk. "I already checked."

Nick stared at her. The white stage lights flashed across her face. "What?"

"Stop looking around," she said. "Bird's not here."

10

SKINHEAD REBEL

Sunday evening Nick was back at the Sunrise Diner with Austin, but this time Victoria and Bird had actually showed up. Nobody wanted to go to the Cro-Mags show at the 321, but Nick kept bugging them. Bird said skinheads were coming down from New York, and another gang was coming up from Philadelphia. "It'll be a fracas. A regular fucking melee."

"But Mike Skin and his crew will be there," said Victoria. She showed them the crude spider web drawn with black marker on her elbow. "It means we're serious. He's got one just like it. He'll look out for me and my friends."

They were all picking from one big plate of cheese fries. Their water glasses were empty. The waitress had put their check down a long time ago and never came back. There was no place else to go and the table next to them kept playing Aerosmith songs on the tiny jukebox so finally they all said, screw it let's go.

On the way out, a table full of preppy teenagers cocked their heads at them and laughed.

Austin said, "Yeah, you're funny, too." Then he stared them down until they looked away and pretended to be talking about something else.

* * *

They had to wait in line to get into the 321, but when they got to the door the bouncer waved them on without frisking them. "I know them," he said to the other bouncers huddled in the alcove like football players crowding the sidelines. "Let 'em through."

They'd never seen the other bouncers before: all broad-chested young guys in orange t-shirts.

"Well, that was weird," Bird said. "When did they hire like five hundred more meatheads?"

Inside, people lined the bar and crowded the walkways. Skinny young men in mohawks, a few boys with tattered clothes and hair like barbed wire, pale-faced Goth girls. And skinheads. Many, many skinheads. Muscular skins with no shirts, the cuffs of their jeans rolled to the tops of combat boots. Sullen skinheads in identical olive green flight jackets. Even Nazis, moving as if they were tied together at the waist, awkward and stiff in long-sleeved brown shirts buttoned to the neck.

The opening act was already on stage. A local band they'd never heard of: four skinny teenagers in sneakers and baggy shorts thrashing beneath the white lights. The pit was a chaos of flailing arms and bobbing heads.

Nick, Austin, Bird and Victoria took a spot in the middle of the floor, facing each other in a circle so they could see what was coming from any direction. Nick said he'd seen deer standing like this on the side of the road and Austin sneered. "I never seen a deer." With his boyish face and spiked-up black hair, whenever he curled his lip he looked to Nick like the world's angriest ten year old.

Bird lit up a cigarette and told Nick he had to get out of the boondocks. It was the first time she'd said something directly to him since showing up. She wore her denim jacket, a tartan kilt and black combat boots. He'd been expecting her to look different somehow, but it had only been three months.

She noticed him staring at her jacket. "It's here." She pointed at the Kafka pin on the upper part of her sleeve, the only spot where there was room.

Victoria shivered and eyed the crowd. A chilly autumn night, but she wore only a bicycle chain necklace and a long black dress that made her look even taller than she was. Part of her new look for

Mike.

"No Oz tonight," Bird said.

"Austin's straight edge now," Nick said. He couldn't figure out anything else to say to say to her. It had been so long since they'd last seen each other and she hadn't said a word all evening about herself or how she was doing.

Bird snorted. "And Ronnie Reagan's a communist."

"No. He's serious. At least, he seems to be."

"He's tired of trying to figure out his own shit. He's just looking for a cage that fits."

She looked up at him, the corners of her mouth turned up in bemusement. Her brown eyes looked black in the dim light. It felt like they were back in their spot at the bar on the Sunday matinee shows.

"It's good to see you," he said.

She rolled her eyes. "*Duh*, of course it is."

He wished he could leave with her right now, go anywhere, even back to the stupid diner. Something was off again. The night felt fractured, like a piece of broken pavement he knew he'd eventually trip over.

Bird turned to light her cigarette and accidentally elbowed a skinhead in the back. One of the gang in the flight jackets. He turned on her. "Hey," he said, glaring down.

Bird widened her eyes like a startled little kid. "What? I didn't do anything."

The guy cursed under his breath and walked away. Bird's innocent face fell away like a mask dropping and the usual scowl returned. "Night of the living morons."

On stage, the scrawny singer paced back and forth. "Stay cool!" he shouted. "We can't self-destruct now."

A shirtless skinhead put a fist in Austin's back and pushed him out of the way. Austin glared and jerked his hands from the pockets of his black leather jacket.

The skin leaned into his face. "Don't even think about it, dumbass." The skin's shoulders were thick and broad, welded to his neck. Austin lowered his gaze when three other skins came up to stand behind the guy.

One of the others said to Victoria, "What the fuck you doing with them?"

She crossed her arms so the spider web tattoo was visible. "I'm looking for my boyfriend. His name's Mike Skin."

"You know how many fucking Mike Skins are here?"

Bird watched the three skins walk away. She exhaled a huge puff of cigarette smoke she'd been holding in. "You know what's wrong with those guys? They don't close their eyes when they laugh." She patted the top of her head. "If I'd known they were taking over I would've brought my clippers."

"I didn't know," Nick said. "I really didn't know."

The band stopped playing. The lead singer said, "That's it! We're leaving. Come on! Ratpacking's for pussies!"

The skinheads up front charged the lead singer in a wave, leaping over the bouncers crouched at the edge of the stage. The bouncers shoved and they tumbled back into the crowd. The singer stalked off the stage. The bass player and the guitarist put down their guitars and followed him.

"Hope you like drum solos!" Bird shouted at the crowd.

Victoria fingered her razor blade earrings. "He's not here. Mike's not here." She chewed at her lower lip.

"Great boyfriend you got there," Nick said.

Austin's head swiveled left and right. "They shut the side doors."

"And there's no room to hide under the bar," Bird said.

"And none of the straight edge guys showed." Austin snorted. "Chickenshits."

Nick leaned into him. "I have to take a piss."

Austin raised an eyebrow. "Have fun."

"I'm not going by myself."

Austin nodded. "Go ahead. I'll follow in a minute so we don't look like fags."

Nick worked his way through the crowd and ducked into the men's room. Three skins in flight jackets were crowded into the only stall. One glared over his shoulder. Eyes down, Nick unzipped at the urinal. His fingertips were cold and numb. The smell of stale urine was so strong he could taste it at the back of his throat. He willed himself to piss but there was a vise on his bladder. He took a deep breath and stared down at the wet cigarette butts. The back of his neck burned. The skinheads laughed. Nick gritted his teeth. He wanted to piss all over them, piss in their faces. It would be worth it.

But nothing was going to happen.

He flushed, needlessly, and left, the skinheads whooping after him.

He ran into Austin and slapped him in the chest. "Thanks a lot! What happened to you?"

Austin glared over at a group of shirtless skinheads fading into the crowd with backward glances at the two of them. "Forget it. We gotta find Mike Skin."

Victoria and Bird were still in the same spot. Bird was flicking her lighter over and over, but had no cigarette. Victoria had tears in her eyes.

"I'm sorry, Vic," Nick said. "I'm sure he'll show up."

"Fuck him," she said. "Some guy just shoved his hand up my ass." She held up her fist to show him the fresh cut across her knuckles. "I punched him in the teeth."

A skinny teenager with long hair ran past, pale-faced and jittery. Three skinheads followed, gazes locked on him, mouths set in tight firm lines.

Nick pulled Austin over. "Let's split."

"*You* wanted to come here."

"I know."

"*You* wanted to see this band."

"It's not worth it. Let's go."

Austin scowled, eyes hard. "Don't roll over like that."

Nick shrugged.

"What is that?" Austin mimicked the shrug. "You come all the way here just to leave?"

"No. I came all the way here and now I'm *deciding* to leave."

"You're not deciding. You're giving up." Austin poked him in the chest. "What's this? What does this pin say? Tell me without looking."

Next to his 7 Seconds pin another read *don't let 'em grind you down*. He recited the line to Austin. "But that isn't about here," Nick said. "It's about out there."

"Yeah, that's convenient. Hope that works for you."

Over Austin's shoulder, he saw the long-haired kid drop to the ground among the three skinheads. "This is stupid," Nick said. "It's not worth it. It's pointless."

"No, man, this *is* the point. Where else we gonna go, dude? We can't even eat in a diner without somebody giving us crap. And now we're supposed to take crap from these stupid fat shits, in our own fucking club?"

"Fascists. Not 'fat shits.'"

"Whatever! Fuck them," Austin spat the words like he was gagging on them. "What'd you want to do about it? Grab a magic marker and write lyrics on the walls? What good is that gonna do?"

Nick felt his face go hard. More skinheads gathered in front of the stage. Some hopped up and down, hands rigid at their sides. Finally, he said, "Go ahead. I'll watch your back."

Austin headed for the crowd in front of the stage. Nick followed. Bird and Victoria linked arms and backed into the nearest wall. Bird held up a hand and waved at Nick with one finger.

The house lights went down again and the stage lights came up as the Cro-Mags took the stage. They looked exactly like the audience: jeans, no shirts. The DJ came on over the loudspeakers, his voice tight. "Listen. We heard—listen, there's been some static tonight. Let's keep it cool and we'll all have a good time, all right?"

Boos came up from the crowd.

"Shut up, you fascists!" Austin yelled. The people around him shifted, shuffled their feet and moved away. A cold void opened inside Nick's stomach. He buttoned up his jacket to keep it from getting torn off in the pit.

The drummer counted off and the guitars snarled and the bass and drums thumped in their chests like a second heartbeat. Austin punched Nick's arm. "Come on!" he shouted.

Austin pushed his way to the edge of the pit and jumped into the swirl of flailing arms and legs. Nick saw the shadows of shirtless skins gliding through the crowd towards him. Their shoulders didn't move when they walked. Their heads didn't bob.

He pressed through the people lining the edge of the pit, one hand outstretched to grab Austin and pull him away. A tall skinhead stepped in his path and stared down. Sweat ran in rivers down the skinhead's face. His eyes were blank. Nick lowered his arm. The skinhead smiled without closing his eyes and turned his back, blocking the view. Nick rose up on his toes.

Austin was thrashing in place, a frantic pogo, the chains on his leather jacket jumping. One skinhead pressed a hand between his shoulder blades and pushed. Austin pitched forward, palms touching the floor, then righted himself and spun, swinging blindly, one arm arcing over his head, the black leather looking for a moment like liquid, like a whip of black oil falling. The skinhead dropped, clutching his face. Then Austin disappeared behind a wall of bare white backs. Fists rose and fell like pistons. Against the glare of the stage lights, the shadows of shaved heads and raised fists swarmed and multiplied until it seemed to Nick, as he stood there frozen, watching, that the entire world was nothing but skinheads.

11

ETCHED IN FLESH

Victoria sat in the back corner of the emergency room, holding a cold compress to one eye. Her black dress was torn down the left side, black lace bra visible, finger-length bruises around her breast dark red against pale skin. A nurse came by and offered a blanket and she mumbled "thank you" without looking up. When she pulled the blanket around her, Nick saw some of her fingernails were broken and jagged.

Bird was turned sideways in the plastic chair, cursing to herself in a low monotone. Every time she moved, she winced. Dark mud stained the back of her jacket. The fabric around the elbows was split open, tiny white threads dangling out of the torn denim.

The nurse came to Nick. "Do you need to get checked out, too?"

"No, I think I'm OK."

He wanted to put his head through the nearest window, then just tear his face into pieces on the shards. The look she'd given him as she walked away.

He'd seen everything.

Austin dragged across the floor by the collar of his jacket, legs curled to his chest to ward off kicks. Others—some skinheads, some not—had shoved Nick aside as they rushed past to get in their free shots. Victoria had punched the skinhead nearest to her in the back of the head, shouting *he's one of us* but the skin only laughed and jerked an elbow back into her face.

Bird had crouched low and worked her way into the crowd and tried to grab Austin's arm, but one of the Crew wrapped his arms around her and tossed her into the air. That was when Nick had finally moved: when he'd seen the yellow flash of Bird's spiked hair as she fell backwards into the storm of punches and kicks. He tried but couldn't get to her. Then the bouncers had shoved everybody out the one door, all of them crushed together, clutching each other to keep from falling over, stumbling, tripping, scattering across the parking lot. Bird went down again, face first, everyone else was so much bigger than her, and he pushed his way toward her and she held onto him for a second, fingers clutching the sleeve of his army jacket, then she pushed him away and ran back into the crowd.

At last, he rose from the stiff plastic seat and went down the hall to where the beds were.

Victoria called, "They don't want us back there, Nick."

He kept going.

A blue curtain was drawn around the bed. He could hear Austin's mother and father behind it: whispers that sounded like the same question repeated over and over. Nick had never seen them before the emergency room. His mother was small, with a dour, pinched face. She wore a dark green sweat suit and gold earrings. His father had on a sweater and tweed jacket even though it was eleven o'clock on a Sunday night. When they'd first arrived at the hospital they'd gone right up to Bird. "What happened to our son?" They'd glared down at her and she'd tried to return the glares but her lower lip had trembled and all she could do was point down the hall.

Nick froze, hand reaching for the curtain. The parents fell silent.

"This wouldn't happen if you freaks just led normal lives and left our son alone." That's what Austin's mother had said to them, before rushing back here.

The curtain parted. Austin's father stood in front of Nick,

blocking the way. He held an empty box of tissues. "What is it?" He had Austin's broad forehead and thick eyebrows, the same sullen stare.

"How is he?" Nick's voice sounded small. He glanced past the man's shoulder. Austin sat propped up, an IV stand beside his bed. White bandages across his nose and under his chin. His eye sockets were purple, swollen pouches. Nick couldn't tell if his eyes were open or not.

"Look, kid." Austin's father spoke slowly, in a hard, dull voice, as if each word were a nail he was hammering in. "The only smart thing you can do right now is get your ass home."

"But . . ."

Austin's father clenched his jaw. He wouldn't look Nick in the face even though they were inches away from each other.

"I didn't." Nick's voice quivered. He wanted to say he was sorry, that he wished it had been him. But Austin's father didn't want to hear any of that. His shoulders slumped and he bowed his head as if in confession. "I didn't *do* anything," he said weakly.

At night, awake, his legs twisted up in the bed sheets, he could almost see it. The way it should have been.

His fingers claw at Austin's jacket, grasping a handful of leather. The muscles across his back straining as he lifts Austin to his feet. Hands pulling and tearing at his field jacket as he shoves his way through the skinheads. The punches pounding on his shoulders, his back, around his ears as he drags Austin to the door, where Victoria and Bird wait, unscathed. Austin slapping the top of his head. *Thanks, dude, thanks.*

He could almost see it. What should've happened.

Two days later, on a cold, gray afternoon, Nick sat in the passenger seat of Victoria's Crown Royal. She said, "They broke his nose. And his one eye is still all swollen up. And some of his front teeth were chipped. And he says his ribs are really sore."

She was driving slowly, leaning over the steering wheel to read house numbers. "His lip was cut really deep. I guess from the steel-toed boots. He wouldn't tell me how bad it was. It was hard to understand what he was saying, like he couldn't move his mouth."

"You just passed it, Vic," Bird said.

She wheeled the car around in a slow U-turn. "I wish he'd never mouthed off to those guys."

"That's no reason to kick his ass," Bird said. "He didn't do anything wrong."

"I know."

They were heading to Austin's to drop off his leather jacket. Bird had taken it home from the hospital and wiped off the dirt and bootprints, but she didn't want to drive over there by herself. She sat in the back, smoking a cigarette, the other hand clutching the jacket laid across her lap like she thought someone would take it away. Nick sat up front. He didn't say a word until they pulled up to a sprawling two-story gabled house with a curving brick walkway. It was a windy autumn day. Red and yellow leaves blew across the lawn.

He grabbed the door handle. "I'll go in."

"No, I'll go," Bird said. "At least they kind of know me. I went to school with him."

"They're going to go off on whoever knocks on the door. Might as well be me."

"No." She tossed her cigarette out the window. "I'll do it."

"Let him go if he wants," Victoria said. "Don't try to apologize, Nick. They don't want us here."

Bird handed him the jacket.

"Well, I'm not going to just drop it and run," he said. "I should say something."

He looked up at the windows. Maybe Austin was looking down at them right now. "You think he'll talk to me?"

Victoria shook her head. "I don't think he wants to talk to anybody." Tiny red veins crisscrossed the corner of her left eye. A dull yellow bruise veiled her cheekbone.

"Tell him we don't care what he looks like," Bird said. "He can't get any uglier."

Nick rubbed his face and sighed. They were quiet for a while, staring at Austin's huge house.

"He never took me home," Victoria said. "I guess he didn't want me to see this."

"Yeah," Nick said. "He seemed so hardcore."

"He was hardcore. Where you come from doesn't matter."

"*Is* hardcore, you losers," Bird said. "He's not dead." She swung open her door. "Fuck it, gimme the fucking jacket. I'll go."

A minute later she came pacing down the winding brick walkway, stiff-backed, eyes fixed on the ground. She slumped down in the back seat and thrust her fists deep into the pockets of her jacket.

"I gave it to his mom. Motherfucker wouldn't even come downstairs."

The finance manager sat behind his desk, staring at spreadsheets. In his left hand, he held a smoldering cigarette, in his right, a red pen. His name was Don, Donald, Donnie—something like that. Nick had only been with this company for a week and managed not to talk to anybody except to get his assignments for the day.

Donald made an X on a line in one of the spreadsheets, took a drag on his cigarette, hacked out a rattling cough. He made another X. He didn't look up at Nick, sitting across from him.

Nick watched the clock on the wall. How many times had he sat like this? How many offices? The dull waiting.

Six and a half minutes passed.

"All right then," Donald sighed, raising a long slack face. He coughed a few more times. "This is absolutely the worst work I've ever seen. Frankly, it's crap. Makes me wonder what you've been doing all week."

Nick pointed at the spreadsheets. "That. I've been doing that."

"Not anymore. You're out."

"No shit?"

He fixed his tired, dogged gaze on Nick. "No shit."

Nick scraped back his chair to stand up.

"Get your timesheet to me," Donald said. "I'll sign it and you can go."

Nick paused. This had been his first temp job in months. On the first day, before he'd walked in and seen the rows and rows of desks and bowed heads, heard the whir of calculator tapes, he'd felt almost eager to start, to finally fill the tiny hollow need that had been gnawing at him. He hated to acknowledge it—wasn't it stupid that he should feel this void over something he didn't care about? But he wanted a job. He wanted a paycheck.

Donald had already gone back to the spreadsheets, marking, smoking, and coughing. Nick hesitated, still in his seat. "I can do better."

Donald raised his head. A slow rusty pivot. "Can't afford to find out."

"I can fix this tonight. Two hours, probably. Three at the most."

"Do you even know what you did wrong?"

"Yeah."

Nick rose and picked up one of the sheets. He explained how he had misclassified the expenses, mixed them up with fixed assets; how he'd prorated the amounts he couldn't classify, then tried to cover his mistakes by spreading the balances around. He'd been lazy and tried to cheat his way through.

"Well." Donald sighed heavily. "Like I said, I can't afford to pay you to fix something that should've been done right the first time."

"I'll stay tonight. And I won't put it on my timecard."

Then he told Donald all the things the clerk before him had done wrong. How his data was screwed up from the start. "And I'll set it up so next week's run will be better than what you guys did before," Nick said. "To show you how next week it can be done in half the time."

His voice was confident, firm, as if he'd rehearsed it. Maybe he *had* said something like this, once, in Deborah's office. It all seemed familiar.

"One more week?" Donald said.

"Yeah."

He scratched his chin and stared at Nick. Not contemplating his decision—Nick could tell he'd already made up his mind. He was pretending to think it over so he could make Nick stand there longer, make him sweat a little more.

"Well, if you're that desperate," Donald said finally. "Go ahead. You can't do any worse."

Nick felt his face burning. He leaned over the desk and gathered up the rest of the spreadsheets.

Donald shook his head, "You must really be in a hole to do a song and dance like that for three fifty an hour!" He laughed, exhaling a cloud of smoke into Nick's face.

Nick kept his hands on the desk. He inhaled deeply and forced out the deepest cough he could muster. Drops of white spittle dotted the spreadsheets and Donald's shirt. Donald's mouth dropped open. He looked down at his shirt.

"Sorry," Nick wheezed. "It's the smoke."

When he got home three hours later, his mind as thin and vacant as a tin box, his mother told him that the temp agency had called. "You don't need to go back. They'll mail your last check." She shook her head. "Were you even trying?"

Victoria slipped off her long black coat. The silk had felt cool and soft when Nick hugged her. They were on the back porch of Rat's ranch house. He leaned against the wall, in the shadows. The wall vibrated with the thump of the music playing in the basement. Victoria laid the coat over a nearby lawn chair. The light from the kitchen window shone on her shaven head and bare upper arm. She ran her fingers over the coat. It was brand new, she'd told him. Paid for, not ripped off.

"What happened there?" He touched a wide, red scrape on one elbow.

"Mike's spider web. It was stupid, so I washed it off. It wasn't a real tattoo, so I scrubbed it with a brush and lots of soap." She folded her arms, cupping the elbow in her palm. "Everybody lets me down," she said quietly.

He rubbed his face. "Yeah."

Down in Rat's basement a few minutes before, everybody had been bouncing around and running into each other to a Fugazi album, but all Nick could see was Austin swinging wildly, face bloodied, surrounded by skins. Even as he'd been dragged across the floor of the 321, he'd kept swinging. That's why Nick had come up here, to get the image out of his mind, and Victoria had followed.

She put a hand on his chest. "He's not mad at you. No one expected you to stop a whole army of skinheads."

"All right." He wasn't sure he believed her.

She wrapped her arms around him and hugged. He buried his face in the soft hollow between her neck and shoulder. Held her tightly, his eyes squeezed shut. He wished she would drag her fingernails down his back the way she used to. Etch trails of blood in his skin, use her fingers like hooks to pull him back down to earth, but she only patted him lightly, her voice a whisper in his ear. "It's OK, Nick. It's OK. Relax."

He pulled back and touched the side of her face. "Thanks."

She smiled. "We'll look out for each other, right?"

"Of course." He nodded. "How're you doing?"

She bit her lower lip. "You know I'm into more than modeling now, right?"

"Crow said something about it. But I didn't know if she was just making it up."

"It's just a few guys. It's through a service, so it's a little safer."

"Victoria . . ." He sighed and shook his head. "Are you sure about this?"

She fixed a level gaze on him. "I'm fine. I know what I'm doing."

"OK. All right."

"I got enough of a hard time from Bird. I really can't handle more from anybody else."

He leaned back against the cold aluminum siding and tried to affect a casual stance, thumbs hooked in the pockets of his jeans. "How's she doing?"

She looked him up and down skeptically. "What happened with you two?"

"Nothing. Absolutely nothing, believe me." A wind blew across the lawn, rustling the dead leaves, and he folded his arms against the chill. "Why?"

"She stopped making jokes about you. Whenever your name comes up, she just gets quiet."

"I couldn't tell you." He shrugged. "We don't talk."

"She doesn't talk to me much anymore either. She's not happy with my lifestyle choices, I guess." She went over to a lawn chair and sat, clasped hands held between her knees, shoulders slouched. "I think she's going to move out on me. She already took her paintings down."

He recalled what she'd said about Bird when they had first met.

She looks out for me. Somebody has to. "You going to be OK?"

"Sure," she said, without conviction, then shrugged. "But it's better having her around, you know?"

"I know."

Victoria bit at her lower lip again. "She keeps me sane."

"Yeah." He stared down at his boots. A dead leaf was caught in the laces. "She's good at that."

In the bathroom mirror in the morning, he fixed the knot of his tie. Another temp gig: this time all the way down in the business district in Philadelphia, an hour and a half's train ride away. File clerk in some data research company. He could already taste the paper dust. His face was clean-shaven and smooth, a mild red razor burn along the jaw line. He cinched the knot and ran his palm across his head to smooth out his hair. When he went to these jobs, he flattened out the spikes and combed his hair to the side. It made his face look long and naked, eyes wide as if perpetually startled. He covered his face with his hands, only his eyes exposed, and stared in the mirror. Pulled down on his cheeks, stretching the skin over his cheekbones. Such an eager-to-please face. An obedient, anonymous face. One to be stepped on. Stepped over.

He pictured that skinhead's face. The one who'd blocked him from reaching Austin. The smug, dull stare. The dumb certainty of someone who'd always gotten his way. That was what had momentarily frozen Nick. Faced with the thoughtless confidence of a human being who does not, will not, cannot think—at work, at the club, wherever—he always felt powerless. Somehow the idiot had known that. Knew he wasn't even worth punching.

He checked his watch. He was going to be late. He looked in the mirror one last time at the face that was not his. He balled his right hand into a tight fist and punched himself as hard as he could, knuckles striking the cavern of one eye socket. Stars flashed behind his eyelids. Yes, he thought. That was the right thing. He leaned on the formica counter to steady himself. His skull throbbed. His stomach twisted. It was the least he deserved.

In the kitchen that evening, his mother said, "You have to stop going to these concerts." She was wrapping an ice pack in a wet towel.

"Mom. I can do it."

A pot of boiling water for spaghetti bubbled on the stovetop. She gently held the pack against his swollen cheek while trying not to look at his face.

"Mom, I can take care of myself."

She put one hand on his upper arm and held the ice pack in place. His father watched from the doorway, trying to see over her shoulder, grimacing.

Their worry pressed against him, but this time he submitted to it. Let them be who they were. His mother's fingers dug into his arm. She was trembling, a brittle shivering like bare tree branches in wintertime.

At the Mekons show that Friday, no one thrashed and there was no pit. There were no skinheads. The Mekons were an older English band that played angry pub songs. The stage was crowded. Three guitarists, a female backup singer, bass, drums, keyboards, even a woman with a fiddle. They laughed a lot between songs. The singer tried to get the tiny crowd to whistle a tune along with him and when the band started the next song, playing over the audience's chirping, he shouted, "Oi! We're whistlin' 'ere!"

They were good, but it felt strange not getting hit in the back—not even once. They closed with "Where Were You?" The more the people around Nick bobbed their heads and bounced in place, the more he wanted to be knocked to the ground, trampled on, stomped beneath steel-toed combat boots.

As soon as the band left the stage, he wheeled for the exit, head down. There was only silence and his bedroom at home, but there was nothing for him here, either.

Quick footsteps came up behind him as he walked to his car. "Hey, loser."

It was Bird. Denim jacket and ripped-up jeans with black tights underneath, her hair longer up top, but still spiked and looking like twisted silver snakes in the white glow of the streetlight.

"Whoa. I thought you were in Philadelphia."

"Not tonight. I'm with Crow and her gang." She took a drag on her cigarette. "They went to buy some weed."

"Were you guys inside?"

"Back bar. I couldn't take the fiddle. You really need to get a fake ID, Prettyboy."

"You heard from Austin at all?"

"No."

"Me neither." Nick put his hands in his pockets and shifted his feet. As always, he could not read her face.

She said, "You seen Vicky lately?"

"Yeah. I hope she's OK with the whole new life she's got down there."

Bird rolled her eyes. "Me too. I've seen some of her new friends. Poser hipster assholes."

"How come you never called me back?"

She shrugged and lowered her eyes.

"What've you been doing?"

"My own thing. By myself. That's how I deal." She squinted up at him. "Who did that to your face?"

"I did."

She took another slow drag on her cigarette, considering this. The tip glowed red. "Why?"

"I don't know." He held himself very still. *This is me*, he wanted to say. *The real me*.

Her eyes were hard and dark. He waited—for what, he didn't know. A sarcastic quip. A dismissive shrug. He'd never cared before what anyone thought of him. It was a new and unnerving feeling. Like balancing on a tightrope so high up you can't see the ground.

But she didn't say anything.

"You think I'm pathetic," he said after a while.

"No. You're not." She shook her head. "Did the shiner make you feel any better?"

"Yeah. For a second there, I felt—I don't know—*clearer*. I know it was stupid. But I don't regret doing it, either. That probably doesn't make any sense."

She shook her head again. A police car sped down the street, blue and red lights flashing, but Bird kept watching his face. "No," she said. "I get it."

"You do?"

"Sure. 'Beat my head against the wall one more time.'" A Black Flag song. "But take it from me. Don't make a habit of it."

A rusty Oldsmobile lumbered across the parking lot. "There's my ride." She watched the car roll to a stop. Crow and some others he didn't recognize got out and went into the club. "Guess they think I'm still at the bar."

"Bird."

She turned back to him. "What?"

"What's your real name?"

One corner of her mouth lifted. "What do you care?"

"I want to know."

"Ask anybody. Most of them know."

"Why can't you just tell me?"

She turned her palm down, opened her fingers and let the cigarette drop to the pavement. "It's a secret."

"You just said everybody knows."

She stepped into him suddenly, head cast back, and gazed into his eyes. "It's a secret for you."

He wrapped his arms around her shoulders and pulled her close. She slid her hands underneath his jacket and ran warm palms up his back.

"Your heart's going like a mile a minute," she said.

Her face was pressed against his chest. He kissed her neck. When she looked up again they kissed a long warm kiss and he felt suddenly still and calm for the first time in a long time and when they pulled back he said, without thinking, "I love you."

She blinked. "Huh. That's not something you hear every day." Her brow furrowed, as if she were concentrating very hard.

He lowered his hands, wishing he could jam the words back into his mouth and start over.

But then she said, "Where's your car? It's freezing out here."

The steamed-up windows held the white glare of 321's flood

light, filling the car with a faint silver glow. The engine idled, the heat through the vents a continuous sigh. Both front seats were tilted back. They curled up into each other, slipping off each other's jackets, t-shirts, jeans. Then Bird pulled back, face a blank, lips parted. She touched his mouth. His jaw. His ears. His chest. Her touch was thoughtful. Curious.

She pulled him to her again and held him in a tight hug. "Slow," she said.

He ran a hand along the inside of one thigh. Her skin was soft and smooth. He touched between her legs. They kissed again and he moved his fingers in slow circles. Quiet stifled gasps rose in Bird's throat. Her fingers dug into his shoulders. Then she pulled her hands away.

"Put on one of those little scuba suits," she said.

He snatched up his jeans from the floor and dug into the pockets. He snapped the condom on as quickly as he could. Kneeling before her, he leaned over to kiss her. She reached down and touched him. He saw her do it, but her fingers were so light he couldn't feel them. He kissed her lips, her cheek, her throat. She put her hands on his shoulders, but they lay there like wet leaves. She was too still.

"What?" he said. "What is it?"

She shook her head and turned her face away.

"What happened? What'd I do?"

"You got the wrong girl."

"What?"

"I'm not the one you want."

"Yes. Yes, you are."

"No. You don't know."

She let her hands drop. He backed away and rolled off the condom. Awkwardly, he pulled up his jeans, the steering wheel pressing into his ribs. She pushed herself upright, pulled down her t-shirt and crossed her arms over her chest. He could not see her face against the white stare of the floodlight, just the silhouette of her profile, the long curve of her neck.

"Are you OK?"

She nodded. He struggled to put on his t-shirt, elbows banging the steering wheel.

"I told you I was messed up," she said. "Can't even enjoy a quick roll in the back seat."

"That isn't what—I didn't mean this to seem like some quick roll." He tried to look into her face but she turned away. "You know that, right?"

"I can't find my jacket."

He felt around the floor for the denim jacket.

"You know that, right?"

"Yeah." She put the jacket on her lap and fingered the pins. They winked when she moved them. "You hate me now."

"What? No." He touched her leg, then quickly took the hand away. "Why would I hate you?"

"You do."

"No. What are you saying? I don't understand."

"You hate me now. I know."

12

WINTER

Rat said, "I don't know what everybody's damage is." She'd come up to Nick while he was standing near the stage and started talking before he could even open his mouth. "It's all so fucked up."

She looked even more withdrawn than usual, face hidden beneath a mess of dyed black hair, chin sunken almost into her chest. "Victoria never talks to me anymore. She's like, too cool now for anybody from the suburbs or something. Bird's picking fights with everybody. Crow already left with some asshole. And I never see Austin anymore, even though he used to be at like every hardcore show here. Everything's messed up."

"What's Bird doing?" Nick asked her.

"Mike Skin's new girlfriend was ragging on Victoria and Bird told her to shut her fat, slutty mouth. She tried mouthing off to Bird, so, you know, they had to pull Bird away before she turned her into a real skinhead. I don't know where she is now."

The music on the PA faded and the DJ came on. "All right, Rollins Band up in ten minutes. Folks, let me remind you once again since nobody seemed to be listening the first two times. No. More. Stagediving. No. More. Slamdancing. They'll shut us down if somebody else gets hurt."

Half-hearted jeers went up from the small crowd.

"You think I'm shitting you?" the DJ shouted, spittle sputtering into static. "They'll shut us down. I'm serious. Think about it. Think about your so-called *scene*."

"I never heard him so mad before," Rat said.

"I just figured it out." Nick jerked a thumb up towards the DJ booth. "That's Ronald, isn't it? He does the hardcore show on WPRB."

"Duh, yeah. And works at the record store at the mall, too. He's everywhere."

"Jump" by Van Halen came on over the PA. "I guess that's meant as punishment," Nick said.

"This crowd is so lame." Rat's mascara was smeared. A black tear ran down her cheek and she wiped it away with the back of her hand. "Where did all these stupid jocks come from?"

He couldn't think of anything else to say. He didn't really want to talk.

She crossed her arms and looked around. "I thought we all could go to the diner or something after. We don't do that anymore."

"I don't know, Rat," Nick said. "I don't know if I can."

She said something under her breath, lower lip quivering.

"What?"

"I used to think you were cool," she said. It was the first time he'd heard her raise her voice. "You were the only guy that talked to me for real. Everybody else would go to Vicky or Crow like I wasn't even there." She looked down at her feet as if she were confessing some major sin. "I thought you were cool."

He shrugged, but she kept staring down at the floor, silent. "I'm sorry," he said. "I don't know what's going on with Bird and me . . ."

She turned away and wove through the crowd with faltering steps, shoulders hunched. Nick glanced around. He'd paid at the door, then gone to the front without looking around. Rat was right. Everyone was scattered. Victoria was down in Philadelphia. Mike Skin was in the corner with the other skinheads and some tall, skinny girl with pigtails and a long black dress.

Bird stood with her back to the bar, lips pursed, slowly banging her fists together. Nick walked up to her. They had not spoken since that night in the parking lot.

"What's the matter?" he asked.

"Bored! *So* bored," she said in time to the beat of her fists.

People pressed around them, waving down the bartenders.

"Way too many assholes in here tonight." Bird rolled her eyes. "I heard these morons saying that if Rollins doesn't do Black Flag songs they're gonna rush the stage."

"Stupid shit." He searched her face for anger or indifference or any sign of what he had done wrong that night. But she was talking to him the way she always did, as if nothing had ever happened.

She glanced over his shoulder. "Hold on a sec. I'll be right back." Jaw set, she walked off.

"Fine." He leaned on the bar. Maybe she didn't want to talk to him. He waved down the bartender and ordered a Coke, but the young man stared off at something behind Nick.

"Uh, dude . . ." He pointed. "Is that your friend?"

Nick turned. Bird was up near the stage yanking a tall blonde girl by one pigtail and slapping her in the face. It was Mike Skin's new girlfriend. Bird planted her feet apart and drew a fist back, but two bouncers jumped in and pulled them both towards the side door. Nick pushed through the crowd and followed.

Bird tried to leap blindly past the bouncer, her blue bandanna pulled down over her eyebrows in the scuffle, and screamed, "All skinheads must *diiiieeee!*" Some cheered, but most of the crowd scattered as Mike Skin and some of the other skinheads surged forward. Bouncers in orange t-shirts leaped down off the stage. The lead one shouted, "That's it! That's it!"

Nick bent forward and charged in. No hesitation this time. A thick arm wrapped around his throat and lifted him so that his toes barely touched the ground.

A bouncer's voice near his ear said, "Take these two out the other door, right?" and the lead bouncer snapped back, "I don't give a shit, Larry, let 'em kill each other."

And then Nick was shoved outside into the winter chill with Mike Skin and five other skinheads. Bird was around somewhere but he didn't want to turn away to look for her. One of the bouncers growled to the other, "I'm so tired of this shit, Tom." Then slammed the door shut.

Nick said, "Well, come on, you fucking assholes. Let's go."

The skinheads stared, fists on hips. They all looked exactly the same: dark blue jeans rolled up to the top of black combat boots, red suspenders, white t-shirts. Bare arms roped with muscle.

"You hear this idiot?" one said to Mike Skin. They all seemed to be waiting for him to tell them what to do.

Nick felt like he was back in front of that skinhead from the gang that had beaten up Austin. These guys were all the same. It wasn't muscle or even hair-trigger rage—it was sheer stupidity that gave them strength. They were never going away. They'd stay here forever, never changing, because they couldn't imagine anything else, or make any other choice. That was the only power they had. They were dumber than everybody else.

"Stupid fucking jock retards," he barked, fists clenched at his sides. "Stupid fucking fascist morons."

He knew he couldn't fight one, much less all of them, but his voice kept booming out of his chest. Maybe he was just as dumb as they were, but he couldn't stop himself.

Two of the skinheads walked slowly around behind him. Mike Skin stepped up, so close Nick could see his crooked teeth, the dull gray eyes. "You're Victoria's friend, right?" He was lean and tall, and spoke quietly, as if they were comrades confiding in each other.

Nick had to look up to talk to him. "Yeah."

"Then don't be stupid, all right?"

"You're the one to tell me what 'stupid' is?"

Mike Skin frowned. "What's your problem, man? You wanna die?"

"Yeah, actually I do."

Mike Skin leaned back, head cocked, eyeing Nick like some indecipherable puzzle. The parking lot was silent except for the muffled clatter of drums, the thudding of a bass from inside the club.

"You ratpacked Austin," Nick said. "What the hell did he ever do to you?"

One of the skinheads behind him said, "That wasn't us."

"It doesn't matter," Nick said. "You're all the same. You act like this is your club, but when those other skins come in you don't do a fucking thing to stop them."

Mike Skin said, "Go home, dude. Get the fuck out of here."

A cold wind blew across the lot. Nick let out a long exhale, breath rising in a cloud of mist. "No."

Mike Skin's frown deepened, but Nick could tell it wasn't anger. He was calculating whether this was worth the effort. Finally, he nodded to the others and turned away. "Let's go."

No punches. No shoves. Nothing. Nick's entire body was wound so tight, he felt as if he were teetering over a steep drop.

"Your girlfriend throws a better punch than you," one skinhead said as he passed.

Staring down at the gravel, he unclenched his fists. He'd wanted to go down swinging, the way Austin had. Not like this.

"You boys had your fun?" Bird stood by the closed door, arms folded. "Ready to go home and jerk each other off now?"

The skinhead bent and shouted into her face, spittle flying, "Shut up, stupid cunt!"

"Yeah, yeah, yeah," she muttered, looking down.

All the skinheads disappeared around the side of the club, except for Mike Skin, who lingered at the corner. He seemed to be waiting for the others to leave. "Tell Victoria to call me," he said to Nick in a low voice.

"I, uh . . ." Nick coughed. His throat felt raw. He had no voice left. "I don't talk to her too much."

"I didn't ask if you guys talk. Tell her to call me."

He disappeared around the corner. Bird wiped her face with the back of one hand, then straightened her bandanna. She pulled a cigarette from a pocket and put it in her mouth, then pulled a lighter from another. But she couldn't get it to spark. Her hands were trembling. "Looks like I picked a good night to quit smoking." She lifted the flap of her chest pocket and slid the cigarette back in.

"What happened with Mike's girlfriend in there?" Nick's whole body kept jangling like someone was shaking him from the inside.

"She called Vicky a whore. I had to do something. She only said it because Vic wasn't here to kick her ass."

"You really nailed her."

Bird let out a goofy laugh. "I know!" She grinned. "It was fun!"

Nick laughed at her and she punched his shoulder.

"Uh oh, look out," he said, raising both hands to defend himself.

She danced around, peppering him with punches until he finally grabbed her. They wrestled around the parking lot, laughing, boots kicking up gravel. Then they separated and took deep breaths. He looked around. It was a cold, clear night, the stars like tiny pin pricks in the black sky. "What're we supposed to do now?"

She glanced back at the front doors. "I might be able to get us back in. Depends on who's working the front." But she didn't move from her spot.

"I called you," he said. "I left messages."

"I'm sure they got recorded over. Vicky's a popular girl these days."

"Is that why you never called me back?"

"No." Her dark eyes flashed up at him, then away. "I didn't have anything to say. Sorry."

"I'm not mad. I was just asking."

She zipped up her jacket and shivered. "Let's amble."

They walked down the length of the lot. All the windshields were silver with frost. There was no one else around. Bird said, "Did you like Black Flag with Rollins or with the other singers?"

"With the other singers. Like Keith Morris. But Rollins was cool too. I've seen his band twice already."

"Everybody says he destroyed Black Flag."

"You think so?"

"I don't know." She shrugged. "They weren't as macho before. But Rollins is still cool. He makes it OK to be fucked up."

"I don't think you're fucked up."

She sighed. "The other night to the contrary, yeah, sure."

"I'm sorry. Sorry about that night. I shouldn't have, I don't know. I shouldn't have rushed you."

They turned around and walked slowly back toward the club. Two bouncers came out through the front door and lit cigarettes.

"I'm all grown up," Bird said. "I can make my own decisions. You didn't rush me."

He nodded. "Was that your first time or something?"

"No, it wasn't. My first time happened when I was ten." Beneath the streetlights, her face was as hard and smooth as a statue's. "And I didn't get to make much of a decision then. Obviously."

The bouncers stood with shoulders hunched, smoking and talking quietly. Nick and Bird walked past them toward a ragged patch of grass and a tall wire fence. Nick went to put an arm around her.

"Don't," she said.

He lowered his arm. "That doesn't change anything," he said.

"For me, I mean."

Their boots kicked up gravel as they walked, the rattle of stones echoing. "Just so you know," he said.

"I'm done talking about it."

"OK." After a while, he said, "Want to go back inside?"

"No. I want to keep walking."

She turned and headed back toward the parking lot. He hesitated, hands in his pockets, unsure if he should follow. She stopped and looked over one shoulder.

"Oh," he said. "You meant with me?"

She rolled her eyes. "Yes, moron."

She continued walking and he hurried to catch up with her.

"Did you want to go back in?" she said.

"No. I want to go home and never leave. Just play records and read books for the rest of my life."

One corner of her mouth lifted. "Way to stay strong, Prettyboy."

"I don't know what else to do. Nothing seems to work out."

They walked along the perimeter of the lot, stopped at the abandoned baseball field, turned around and retraced their steps back. The ground was frozen hard as pavement. Beneath the floodlight, the bouncers threw side kicks at each other and laughed. Muffled cheers came from inside the club. The band had just come on. Nick slowed his step to match Bird's shorter stride. He buttoned his army jacket and turned up the collar. She thrust her hands deeper into her pockets. Their breaths rose in white clouds beneath the streetlights.

"I don't think I can be with anybody," Bird said finally. "Like, ever."

13

LAW OF SINES

Monday
          Tuesday
                    Wednesday
Thursday
Friday
The 7:10 R3 SEPTA train from West Trenton.
Yardley
Woodbourne
Langhorne
Neshaminny Falls
Trevose
Somerton
Forest Hills
Philmont
Bethayres
Meadowbrook
Rydal
Noble
Jenkintown
Elkins Park
Fern Rock
Wayne Junction

Then pass through the black tunnels beneath Philadelphia to arrive at Market Street East station at 8:08. Stand up, adjust belts, coats, ties. Shuffle into the aisle, taking turns out the door, bodies alternating like gears meshing, step out into the underground station smelling like the inside of a car engine and move towards the stairs, high heels and dress shoes marching, bodies coming together again at the concrete steps stained and sticky with spit and spilled sodas, the sway of shoulders, purses and briefcases swinging, and then climb the last step and disperse into the wind and noise of the city.

There was more work in the city, and longer assignments, up to months at a time, so Nick had bought a SEPTA rail pass and lined up in the early mornings with the other business people at the train station in Ewing for the hour and a half ride into Philadelphia. The jobs there were just like the ones in the suburban offices, except he was on the fifteenth, or twenty-eighth, or thirty-sixth floor and could not even see the street from his window, only the glass face of the skyscraper opposite reflecting the sky back at him. Somehow that seemed more honest.

The invoices dropped into his box every day and never stopped coming, so it was easy to lose himself in the monotony. If any thought forced him to put his pen down and draw a hand across his eyes he would work that much faster, do more and more invoices, and turn off his thoughts, like turning off lights in a house, one room at a time, until just one was left burning. The one he needed to do his work.

A year passed like this, almost unnoticed except for the changing of the seasons. Heading for his car one sunny morning, the lawns wet with dew, he'd realized it was time to put the wool winter coat away. Sometime later, leaving an office one gray evening, he'd stepped into stifling heat, all the rank city smells suspended in the soggy air, and wondered what happened to spring. Only at these moments did he look up from his life and marvel at how quickly the days slid away.

Everybody's scattered.

On a Tuesday morning in November, he sat on his bed, rubbing sleep from his eyes. He had a few days off before the next job. He listened, for the third time, to Victoria speaking, hushed and low, on his answering machine. She must've left the message yesterday, while he was working. *You should see me. I had to let my hair grow in. My cut was scaring all the guys.*

He hadn't heard her voice in almost a year. He had forgotten how carefully she spoke. Every word enunciated gently, as if she were caressing each syllable with her tongue. *Now I'm whoever they want me to be.* A long sigh. *Motherfucker. Where are you? I've called four times.*

A long pause. In the past, in her messages, he would've heard police sirens, horns honking, shouts. But this time there was only a whoosh of air, like continuous wind. A highway.

I heard it's closed. They shut the 321 down. So. That's gone, too.

He went out to the kitchen and ate a bowl of Cheerios. Then paged through the classifieds, making sure to leave the paper out on the dining room table to show his parents he was still looking. He listened to albums—The Feelies, The Fall, then Rollins Band—but the house still felt too quiet. He read a short story collection, and Camus again, but had to stop and re-read the same passages over.

When the phone finally rang, in the middle of the afternoon, he answered it between the first and second ring. A woman's voice, professional and smooth. "Hello, may I speak to Nick LaBlanche please?"

"This is Nick."

"Nick, hello. It's Ellen from the HR department at Fitzwaters Incorporated. You were here a few weeks ago for the position in the accounting department."

"Yes. I remember." His voice echoed in the empty house, awkward and unsure.

"Well, Nick, I have some great news for you. Everybody on the team was impressed with your credentials and we want to offer you the position. Isn't that great?"

"Oh." He sat down on the edge of his bed. "OK."

"We're prepared to offer you the salary we discussed, as well as the benefits package."

He was stunned. Throughout the interview he'd been taciturn, tight-lipped. He couldn't even remember what he'd said. Only that his answers repeated things he'd heard other people say in his old office. He even mimicked some of the hand gestures from meetings, like rubbing his chin with his fingertips to appear thoughtful, or motioning as he spoke, palm up as if dealing out playing cards. He had seemed to be watching himself as he was interviewed, coaching himself from a distance. *Talk now. Smile now. Stop talking. Nod and smile.*

"Nick? You still there?"

"Yes. I'm here."

"I thought we were cut off for a second. Now, let's run through the details . . ."

They discussed salary and benefits, agreed he would start in one week, then hung up with cheerful goodbyes.

He lay back, still stunned. A real job, finally. He should feel relieved. At least now he could go back to paying his parents for board again. Maybe even get a place of his own. He ran his fingers through his hair, which he'd forgotten to comb. Rubbed his face, felt the stubble on his chin.

He sat up and opened the drawer of the nightstand. Inside were the silver choke chain and all the pins he'd bought at Splat. He shoved them aside, pulled out his address book and dialed Victoria. An automated voice told him the number was disconnected. He hung up, rewound the answering machine tape and replayed her message. She'd never left a number. He put the address book away. He would have to wait for her to call again.

He scooped up the pins with both hands, dropped them on the bed and picked through them, examining each. *PiL. Black Flag. X.* The tape hissed. He'd forgotten to turn off the machine. He bent and reached for the stop button. The machine beeped. Then, one after the other, came the voices from months ago—no, it was a year now. Bird, Austin, Crow, Rat, Victoria, crowding and overlapping each other as if fighting over the phone.

going to the show? guess you already left I'll catch youse there your head up in the pit this time where you at I need a their new album did you get it I don't think he really wants to kick your ass

*meet us outside ok you hear me cause we don't have enough dough
to get in so you're not there so I'm leaving this stupid message so
you suck this is Bird if you didn't know some static so stay the fuck
out of the pit I miss you Nick don't be mad at me it's Bird—again!
forget about calling me back I'm already gone*

The machine went silent, then clicked and whirred as the tape
rewound. He picked up the choke chain and wrapped it around his
fist, twisting one end. The chain tightened and the links bit into his
skin. He held it for as long as he could before placing it back in the
drawer.

Still lost in the voices, he went to the living room, its hardwood
floors creaking. He passed the mural-sized front window, red leaves
scattered across the front lawn, gray clouds low in the sky, and
glimpsed a figure standing at the foot of his driveway. He looked
away. No—that couldn't be her. He looked again. She was really
there. Victoria, standing in his driveway.

He opened the front door just as she stepped onto the porch. Her
pale blue eyes went wide. "So you're still alive," she said, smiling.

Her black leather jacket hung down past her hips. Her hair was
bleached white again, but now it was longer and straighter and fell
into her eyes.

"How did you find my house?"

"I still have your address. We just drove around until we found
it."

Nick looked over her shoulder but there was no car in the
driveway.

"Oh, it was this guy I know. I told him to drop me off up the
street. He's gone. He has no idea which house I went to." She
stepped inside. "But if he comes back don't answer the door and he'll
go away."

They hugged and she kissed him quickly on the cheek. "Close the
door," she said.

In the living room her thigh-high boots sounded like horse's
hooves on the hardwood floors and made her hips swing in
exaggerated arcs. "So this is your house. Nice." She slipped off her

jacket and dropped it on the couch. "Are your parents home?"

"They're at work."

She wore a black mini-skirt and a snug white t-shirt stretched taut across her breasts.

"You lost weight."

"I don't eat." She put her hands on her hips. "Did I lose too much?"

The fullness was gone from her face and there were shadows beneath her eyes.

"No. You look good."

"Love this look." She reached up and mussed his hair. "Yuppie gone psycho."

"It wasn't deliberate." He'd let it grow long again.

She paced through the dining room and into the kitchen, gazing around. He followed her. She looked so out of place here. It reminded him of those collages in the zines he used to pick up at the 321 Club. Random images cut out of newspapers and pasted into scenes where they didn't belong.

She peered out the back window over the kitchen sink, palms on the counter. "No matter where you go, everybody's back yard has the exact same stuff in it."

They stared out at the bare branches of the oak trees and the lawns dotted with soccer balls and folding chairs and lawnmowers. Victoria bit her lower lip.

"I can't believe you're here," Nick said.

She smiled wearily. "Surprise."

"Everything OK—?"

"Yes," she replied quickly.

He took a pitcher of iced tea out of the refrigerator and poured her a glass. "Want to sit down?"

"I'll stand. If I sit I'll collapse." She took a sip and sighed. "That's good." Holding the glass with both hands, she cast her head back and gulped down the rest.

He watched her throat moving up and down. "Thirsty?"

She laughed and delicately wiped her lips with her fingers. "I haven't had anything all day." She picked up the box of Cheerios on the counter and opened it. "Ooh, can I have some?"

"Let me fix you something."

She scooped a handful of Cheerios into her mouth and chewed

quickly, with great concentration. He opened the refrigerator. He wanted to fix her a big meal, to do something to thank her for coming to his house to see him.

"I'm fine with this, Nick. What's down here?"

He followed her down the hall to his bedroom. The high-heeled boots made her walk with exaggerated slowness, shoulders back, spine arched. She stopped in the doorway. "You don't have anything on your walls."

He shrugged. It had never occurred to him. As Victoria gazed around, arms folded, he saw his room the way a stranger would. Bed, nightstand, lamp, tiny clock radio. Record player on the floor. Plastic milk crates filled with albums. A bookcase stuffed with paperbacks. A wooden chair buried beneath a pile of laundry he never got around to folding.

"You just move in?"

"No."

"Oh. What's all that stuff?"

The pins from his dresser were all laid out on the bed. He scooped up some and dropped them back in the drawer. "Nostalgia, maybe," he said.

"Not as many as Bird but you have some good ones." She picked up one and contemplated it. "I'm taking this."

"Do you really think it's closed now?"

"Don't know for sure. You haven't gone to any shows?"

"No. Not since last winter." He put the rest of the pins away and sat on the edge of the bed. "It feels like it never happened."

"It happened. But you can't rewind. You're not that guy anymore."

"I don't know. I feel like I missed something. Like something got by me too quickly."

She sat down next to him and hunched forward, clasped hands between her knees, shoulders slouched. She'd lost the straight-backed, regal posture she'd had when she first walked in. She yawned, both hands over her mouth, then laughed. "Sorry," she said.

Beneath her makeup there were gray circles under her eyes.

Nick said, "You can lie down for a little bit if you want."

"Thanks."

"You sure everything's OK?"

"Why do you keep asking me that?

He shrugged. "You just showing up. It kind of threw me."

She rubbed her eyes. "I'm trying—" She pulled her hand away. "Shit. I still have eyeliner on." She rubbed the dark smudges away by running a finger beneath each eyelid, staring at the ceiling as she did this, her thin red lips parted slightly as if about to sing. "I'm trying to catch up with everyone. But they're all so scattered." She pulled a tissue from the box of tissues on his nightstand and wiped her fingers clean. "Or maybe nobody wants to talk to me."

"No. Why would you think that?"

She rolled the top of one thigh-high boot down over her knee, then bent to try to pull the boot off. She straightened with a groan. "Can you help me?"

He rose. She lay back, propped on her elbows, and lifted her foot.

"Don't look up my skirt."

"I wasn't!"

"I was kidding."

He pulled off one boot and she lifted the other leg. As he slid the other off, neatly folded bills fell to the hardwood floor. He picked them up.

"Oh." She sat up. "I knew I had put that somewhere."

"I don't think I've ever seen a real hundred before."

She held out a hand for the money, then said, "Forget it. Just put it back in my boot." She lay down on her side, head on the pillow, knees drawn up. Her bare thick-muscled legs were smooth and her skin shone as if it were wet. Moisturizer, he guessed. Before, her legs had always been bruised, lined with tiny nicks, with dry patches on the knees.

He sat on the edge of the mattress. She blinked slowly at him, her long bleached blonde hair fanning out over the pillow. She asked what he'd been up to, where'd he gone, who he was seeing.

Every answer was the same. Nothing. Nowhere. No one. He rested his elbows on his knees. The sliding door of the clothes closet in front of him was open. Swirls of dust curled beneath the cuffs of his dress pants. It was so much easier to ignore your life when you were by yourself.

"So," he said. "You haven't talked to anybody?"

She shook her head. "Not really. I've pretty much had to deal with everything on my own."

"I'm sorry. You could've called."

"I thought you'd be mad at me about my job. Everybody else seems to be."

"Well, I hate what you do. But I'm your friend. Always will be."

She raised her head and smiled at him. One of the old smiles, lips closed, creases in the corners of her eyes. Then she put her head down. Her face softened and her mouth loosened. She shivered suddenly, and wrapped her arms wrapped around herself.

"I'll leave you alone," he said.

"You can stay here with me if you want."

He took off his sneakers and lay down beside her. He wrapped his arms around her broad shoulders. Her hair smelled of perfumed hairspray and cigarettes.

"I just want to sleep, though," she said.

"I know. I understand."

A light breeze rattled the venetian blinds. Outside, a distant lawnmower buzzed.

"And don't worry about me. I'm quitting." She leaned her head back on his chest and curled into him. "That guy that dropped me off? He was my very last outcall ever."

He rubbed her shoulder. "Good. I'm glad you're getting out. I was worried about you."

"It's OK," she said slowly. "I'm still here. I'm still me."

She was quiet after that, her breath slow and steady. He felt the muscles in her back relax, her body slowly go heavy. He lay back, his head propped on a folded pillow. He watched the wind moving the blinds.

"What about Bird?" he said finally. "What's going on with her?"

But she was sound asleep, lips parted, hands clasped tightly beneath her chin like a child clutching a cherished doll.

He closed his eyes. So strange to hear someone else breathing beside him. It made everything feel smaller.

Victoria smoked a cigarette out on his front porch, her hair pulled up in a sloppy ponytail, black leather jacket hanging off one shoulder. She had taken one of his pins—the one that read *we are all prostitutes* —and pinned it to her t-shirt. "Much better, Nick."

He had on an old pair of jeans, a gray Hüsker Dü t-shirt and a flannel shirt with its tattered tail hanging out. She'd refused to leave the house with him still in the navy blue sweats. "You look different," he said.

"I washed the makeup off. It's just me now."

Her face was pale and smooth, except for gray hollows beneath her cheekbones and under her eyes. He could tell by the way she was blinking that she wasn't totally awake yet.

"Thanks for taking me to the train station," she said.

"I can drive you to Philly. I don't have to be anywhere."

"Too much shit to clean up the minute I get down there. I want to deal with it on my own."

"All right." He slapped dust off the toes of his combat boots. "I had to dig these out of the back of the closet."

"Those were Austin's, right?"

"Yeah."

"You don't wear them?"

He shook his head.

"He gave them to you," Victoria said.

"Actually, he gave them to you."

She rolled her eyes. "To give to *you*. I don't know why you don't believe that."

"I feel funny wearing them."

"He's not mad at you."

"Did he say that?"

"No. But I can tell. Why do you think he gave you his boots?" She reached over the railing and tapped the ash off her cigarette. "He gave away all his hardcore stuff."

"Why?"

She shrugged. "He's in the army now."

"Really?"

"Yeah. He called me. Right after he got out of army camp or whatever they call it. He likes it."

"Really? He likes taking orders?"

"No. He likes the idea that he can shoot people and not get in trouble for it."

"We never talked. Afterwards, I mean."

"He didn't talk to anybody, Nick."

"Yeah, I know."

"I don't think his face healed right. He still talks funny, like something's stuck in his front teeth."

Nick felt his own face go hard. He unlocked his car and held the door for her. A silver Jaguar, low and sleek, slowed in front of his driveway, then quickly pulled away.

"Must be from Princeton," Nick said. "Nobody has a car like that around here."

Victoria dropped her cigarette and stamped it out with a slow twist of one boot heel. "I think it's Larry."

"The guy that dropped you off?"

"Pretty sure that's his car." She slipped on her jacket. "Let's go. It doesn't matter."

"What the hell? So he's been driving around the neighborhood all day?"

The Jag came back and rolled to a stop in front of Nick's driveway. The car window slid down with a quiet hum. A man with a pudgy face and thinning, salt-and-pepper hair leaned across the seat and looked at them. "Marilyn!" he said. "Marilyn, can I talk to you for one minute?"

Nick looked at Victoria, eyebrows raised.

"It's not like I use my real name," she said quietly.

"Marilyn, please! Just one second!"

Nick walked down the driveway, boots thudding on the pavement. "Get lost, asshole!"

"Nick, it's OK," Victoria said. "Let it go."

He stopped a few paces from the car, a familiar rumbling building in his chest. The man had ruddy skin that sagged like a deflated balloon beneath his eyes and around his mouth.

He waved in Nick's direction. "Look, fella. I just need a word with Marilyn. It's nothing to make a big deal about."

Nick recognized the pompous tone, the perturbed look, immediately. Even the offhand gesture of dismissal. Larry was management.

Victoria said, "Go home, Larry."

"Yeah, Larry." Nick waved a hand. "Go the fuck home."

The man swung open the car door and stepped out. Though he was tall and broad-shouldered, everything about him was sagging and loose. A round belly strained against a mint green polo shirt. A roll of flesh hung over the belt line of his pressed khakis.

Nick angled his body the way Austin had shown him, one foot behind the other at a diagonal, hands low but held in front of him.

Larry stopped at the foot of the driveway. "Marilyn, I just need a few minutes to talk. We can work something out."

Nick shook his head. "Go. Home. Larry."

"Look, fella, this is none of your business. Can't you go inside for a few minutes? We don't have to make this into a problem."

His stomach tightened. His hands were shaking. He bent his knees and bounced on the balls of his feet. He wanted to lunge. "You're in my fucking driveway stalking my fucking friend. So who's the problem here, *Larry*?"

The guy stepped back and put one hand on the open car door, mouth open, eyes wide. Startled. Maybe even afraid. But there was still annoyance in the downward turn of his mouth. Nick guessed he wasn't used to people getting in his way.

Along the driveway Nick's dad had laid down a border of small white rocks. He bent and snatched up three good-sized ones in his left hand.

"What is *wrong* with you?" Larry said, grimacing.

Nick passed one rock into his right, drew his arm back and threw as hard as he could. Larry ducked, covering his head. The rock ricocheted off the Jag's roof with a metallic twang. He took aim and threw another. This one struck the passenger door and left a small, jagged dent in the gleaming metal.

Larry winced. "Hey!"

Nick laughed and rolled the last rock in his palm.

"Are you insane?" Larry shouted. He jumped back into the car, cursing when he bumped his head on the door frame. The Jaguar squealed away, the last rock soaring after it but falling short and bouncing down the empty street. Nick walked back up the driveway on legs that felt like springs. That old freight train feeling barreled through his chest, as if he'd just stepped out of the pit. He clenched and unclenched his fists.

Victoria hadn't moved from beside his car.

Nick laughed. "He looked a lot bigger when he stood up."

She stared off down the road, biting at the corner of her mouth. "There goes my rent."

* * *

They drove out of Hopewell and sped along the curving back roads, passing shadow-filled woods and fields of tall wavering grass. The pounding in his chest had stopped, but now his arms and legs felt heavy. He headed south on Route 31, through Pennington, where the woods grew sparse and finally gave way to parking lots and stores lined up like shoeboxes in a closet. Into Ewing, the road opened up to four lanes and there were traffic lights at every mile.

"The houses keep getting smaller and smaller," Victoria said.

"If we went north they'd get bigger and bigger," Nick said.

"I've been in all kinds of houses. With all kinds of people. I can go anywhere. Be anybody."

"I'd rather just be myself."

"Easy to do if you hardly leave your house," she said flatly.

He turned left onto Olden Avenue into an unceasing tide of cars. On either side of the street huge stores squatted at the end of wide, nearly-empty lots. "So, who's this Larry guy?" Nick said.

"Some executive vice president of whatever. Something like that. He lives outside of Princeton, but he has a little place in the city, too."

"What's his problem?"

"He got too attached. One of those guys that can afford to pay for somebody to pretend to be his girlfriend for an entire weekend. Sometimes they start to believe it. That's why a lot of girls won't do it. All that talking and pretending wears you down."

He looked over at her. "Is he psycho or what?"

"Don't worry about it," she said quietly and firmly. "I'll deal with him on my own." She stared ahead, arms crossed, jaw set tight.

"OK, sorry. Just asking."

The road narrowed to single lanes. The houses were again cramped close together. Passing Cutler Street, Nick said, "We're close to the 321. Want to find out if they're really closed or not?"

Victoria didn't answer.

"Maybe we can pick up some flyers," he added.

She frowned, eyes downcast.

"Victoria?"

"Sure. OK." She flinched slightly, distracted, then nodded. She bent over, back curved like a question mark, to stare down at her feet.

"I really hate these boots," she said.

Nick turned right on Cutler Street and passed the warehouses with the windows boarded up and the check cashing stores and pawn shops with steels bars on the doors. At a street corner a thin black man in a baggy, silver track suit nodded at him.

"Over here," the man said to Nick, cocking his head towards the side street.

Nick drove on. The street was empty. At the familiar tall wire fence, he braked and turned cautiously, ready to navigate the deep craters of the parking lot.

"Whoa," he said, as the car rolled smoothly forward.

The lot had been repaved: not a pothole in sight. He slowed in front of the building. He and Victoria glanced at each other, eyes wide.

"What the hell," Nick whispered.

"Somebody painted it," Victoria said.

The walls of the 321 Club were covered with a clean fresh coat of dark blue paint. No tattered flyers. No spray-paint graffiti. The front door was propped open with a garbage can. An older black man was sweeping out the alcove.

Nick turned back to her. "You want to go in and see what bands are coming up?"

The man called over, without looking up from his broom. "Keep rolling, people. Keep rolling."

Victoria leaned out her window. "Excuse me?"

"Excuse you?" The man leaned on his broom. "You passed what you're looking for. Best turn around."

His blue 76ers cap was pulled down to his eyebrows. It was hard to see his face.

"We just wanted to pick up a flyer," Victoria said.

The man gripped the broomhandle. He had thick hands, knuckles like walnuts. Nick and Victoria bent in their seats and tried to see past him into the club.

"You know Tuff Crew?" the man said. "They're coming in Saturday."

"What the hell's that?" Nick muttered under his breath to her.

"That's hip hop, right?" Victoria asked the man.

"Uh huh. This a hip-hop club, right. But you knew that."

"No. We didn't know that."

The man shrugged and went back to sweeping.

"We used to come here all the time," she told him. "When it was the 321 Club."

With one broad motion, he swept a pile of dirt and paper scraps out the door. "Sure. I know all about that. Red and blue lights up and down the street all night. White kids spray painting all over the walls. White kids in their daddy's car dealing right in front of my house. Picking broken bottles up off the sidewalks every Monday morning." He laughed without smiling. "Wasn't hip hop then, was it?"

"No," Victoria said. "It was something else."

A short drive later, they were sitting on a metal bench on the train platform. The sun had dipped behind the buildings and the sky had turned dark gray. They winced against the strong wind. Strands of hair kept coming loose from Victoria's ponytail and whipped around her face.

"Are you going to talk to her?" she asked.

Nick leaned his elbows on his knees and shrugged.

She pulled the hair back from her face again. "Are you?"

"She doesn't want to talk to me," he said.

"You don't know that for sure."

"Yeah. You're right. All those phone calls I made last year that were never returned. That must've given me the wrong idea."

"You gave up."

"There was no choice. I knew that from the minute I left that Rollins show. She didn't even say goodbye. I don't even know why I tried calling her afterward."

"You should've kept on trying."

"No."

"You have to make an effort sometimes, Nick."

"For what?" He turned to face her. "She didn't want me. That's not going to change."

Victoria narrowed her eyes. "She doesn't want anybody. Or at least that's the story she's been telling herself."

"Have you tried to talk to her?"

"Only once. For her birthday. And that was weird. She barely said a word."

"See."

"No. That's different, Nick. She didn't sound like Bird. Something wasn't right."

"She misses you."

"No." She shook her head. "Not me. She misses *you.*"

"You two were always looking out for each other. I don't think she feels the same without you around."

"I can't do anything for her, Nick. I can't even get my own shit together."

"Is that why she moved out?"

"I guess so. You'll have to ask her." Victoria considered for a moment. She looked away at the people waiting for the train, clustered at the edge of the platform. Men with briefcases. Women in dress suits with sneakers and short white tube socks. She shook her head. "Even the young ones look old."

They were silent for a while. Then Nick said, "I can't believe the place closed."

"I know. Where does everybody go now?"

"No place else around here. They'd have to go to Hoboken or Philadelphia."

"Or just stay home."

"Which is not a real choice," he said. "I should know."

She crossed her arms against the wind and glanced sideways at him. "You seem really different. Compared to this morning, I mean."

He nodded. All day he'd felt like he was slowly awakening from a long slumber. "It's too bad it closed."

She shrugged ruefully. "It wasn't like we were making tracks to get there. Not like before."

The train for Philadelphia wheezed to a stop. She folded her hands on her lap. "Listen. Bird's not as indifferent as she acts. It's just—she was treated like dirt for so long she thinks she *is* dirt. She never came out and said it but I could tell she liked how you listened. I think it made her feel important."

They stood up. Victoria wiped a tear away with the back of one hand. "She's not going to pick up the phone. And her parents never pass on any messages. Go see her. She works at Macy's. Or used to."

"You're kidding."

"I know. It's weird."

They hugged and held on to each other for a moment. Then she kissed him on the cheek. "Tell her I'm sorry," she whispered into his ear.

They waited for the commuters to step off the train, then she got on. Nick watched through the windows as she walked past, then dropped into a seat, black leather jacket pulled around her shoulders. She chewed on her lower lip, a frown etching deep lines in her forehead. Maybe she was thinking about whatever it was she was going home to.

The train rolled forward. The passengers who'd just stepped off waited in a tight row for it to pull away so they could cross the tracks and head to the parking lot. When he waved, Victoria looked up suddenly, as if startled. He kept his hand raised in farewell. She tilted her head back, blinking against the hair falling back into her eyes, and smiled. The same sad, blind smile he remembered from long ago in her bedroom. She waved at him and, as the train pulled away, continued waving at all the people standing on the platform. Some even waved back.

That evening, he came home to find his parents in the dining room. They'd recently started eating at the dinner table again. It still caught him off guard.

He said, "Well, I finally got a job. A real one."

His father clenched a fist. "Yes!"

"Congratulations!" His mother grinned. "I have to admit, we were worried you were never going to work again."

His father nodded, lips pursed in what Nick thought was meant to be a smile. "Some days we weren't even sure you'd leave your room. Let alone go on an interview."

"Some good news for a change." His mother clapped softly, smiling over the tuna casserole at his father.

Nick was stunned. There'd never been much laughter in the house. Was this all they needed to hear to be happy? For a moment, he glimpsed what they must've been like when they were young, before they had a child, bought a big house, even got married. When they were not bent over with worry about him, or worn down to weary silence by their jobs.

Every night after that, no matter what kind of day he'd had, when he came home and his mother said, "How was work today?" he thought of this and always answered, "Good, Mom. No problems."

Nick, it's Victoria. It was wonderful seeing you, but God, you need a haircut. I'm going away for a week. Larry's taking me to Atlantic City. I know. Don't be mad at me. Please. You don't understand.

On the train ride home Tuesday night, or maybe it was Wednesday, Nick closed his eyes to the passing landscape of row homes and strip malls and tried to sleep. He'd been in this new, permanent job for three weeks now and so far it was indistinguishable from all the others he'd had.

In the seat in front of him, two women chattered in quick, high voices that reminded him of sparrows. "Can you believe she said that? Right in front of me."

"The nerve."

"So I waited until the meeting was over. Went right up to her and said, if you think I'm doing your work for you, for absolutely nothing in return, you've got another thing coming."

"You said that? Right to her face?"

"Not exactly in those words. But she got the message."

"Good for you."

"I've worked there too many years to be talked to like that."

The woman repeated the same story, with new details, throughout the entire ride, growing angrier each time she told it. It was always the clerks and secretaries that had these indignant rants on the train. Never the managers. Nothing ever disturbed their smug monotones.

Nick glanced at the others around him. An older woman in a stiff blue suit dozed, spine so perfectly straight she might've been strapped into the seat, chin on her chest, her head lolling back and forth. A gray-haired man flipped through a newspaper, straightening the pages every few minutes with quick shakes as if he were punishing it. Other passengers gazed blankly out the windows. Nick lay his head back and closed his eyes. He remembered the last time he'd gone to ADR, waiting in the lobby to meet with the HR guy to get his last paycheck. The faces of the people that'd been laid off: the lines of worry framing thin, tight mouths. The uncertain, cautious way they walked into a building they used to stroll through as if it were just another room in their home.

The HR guy—Gary—had sat in an office at the far end of a vast, empty maze of cubicles. The blue-white fluorescents in the space were the only lights on the entire floor. Nick remembered walking through the dimness towards the glow of Gary's office, like weaving through the insides of huge machine that had been shut down. An empty engine. When the engine died, they—Gary, Nick, the people in the lobby, the people on this train—would all spill out and scatter, then gather again someplace else, pressed together on rail cars and long crowded highways. Eventually, they would be dispersed again, and, eventually, gather together again. Like some kind of homeless, suburban tribe. Nomads looking for an empty cubicle to fill, a clean desktop on which to put their coffee mugs, their pens, their calculators, their steno pads.

Nick's head lolled and he opened his eyes with a start. He shifted in his seat, staring out at the back yards of the houses rolling past. He was getting close to his stop: the houses were bigger along this stretch and tall trees lined the roads.

Victoria had been fascinated by the commuters at the Ewing station. But then she'd never worked a full-time job, or in an office: it was all a curiosity to her. He thought about her message and the last thing she'd said to him before she left. He had no idea what he would say to Bird if he ever saw her again. Or what she would say to him, if she could see him the way he was right now. What would she do if she were living this life?

"West Trenton! Last stop. West Trenton!"

Nick rose, a sour gummy taste in his mouth. He felt hollow. I can't do this anymore, he thought. Something has to change.

But then he always thought that.

14

FOR WANT OF

The following Monday, Nick rode the escalator down to the first floor of Macy's. Muzak dripped like slow poison from unseen speakers in the ceiling. Downstairs, glass display counters filled the center of the store. The lighting was white and soft. Slender young women with smooth, placid faces arranged wicker baskets full of flowers or bottles of perfume. When they reached beneath the counters, they bent from the hips like ballet dancers.

He moved slowly through the aisles. No way, he thought. Bird must've been playing a joke on Victoria. She wouldn't be caught dead in here.

Passing a cosmetic counter, he heard a low voice say, "Is there anything else you need today?"

A tiny girl with a pageboy haircut was ringing up two white-haired women with big, baggy purses. The girl was dwarfed by the poster behind her of a pale-faced model applying lipstick. Nick recognized the cigarette-worn tone, even though now it was stiff with false courtesy. "For just fifteen dollars more," she said. "You can also have the gift basket, which includes the moisturizer, the potpourri, and the, um . . ." She paused and stared at the ceiling, as if the next word was written up there.

The woman held up a hand. "This is all I need, thank you. No sales pitch, please."

"OK. Whatever."

The girl jabbed at the cash register with one finger. Yes, it was definitely Bird. The round face. The dark serious eyes. But her hair was blonde, not white but straw-colored, with streaks of brown. It hung straight down, framing her face and curving just beneath the jawline. She wore a white silky blouse with broad, flat shoulder pads. It was how all the women at his temp jobs dressed, but on her it looked like a costume.

The old woman said, "This was a sales item, dear. This is not the sale price."

"Whoops." Bird took the receipt back and glanced across the aisle. She looked right at Nick. He opened his mouth but her gaze moved past as if she didn't recognize him.

"Hey, Trudy," she called over one shoulder. "I need a void." She turned back to the register and poked at the buttons. "Stupid thing's not working again."

Nick couldn't help but stare, disappointed. He felt betrayed. But why? Because she was no better than he was?

The women left and Bird let out a sigh. She looked up again, right at him, then cocked her head, one eyebrow raised. "Holy shit," she said flatly.

He came up to the counter. "Hi, *Marla*. How's it going?"

She glanced down at her nametag. "Oh, crap. I would've taken it off if I knew you were coming."

"How are you doing?" he said, seriously this time.

She shrugged. "I'm at the mall. How do you think I'm doing?" She glanced up at his mess of hair. "What're you doing? Shopping for a new comb?"

"I saw Victoria."

"Yeah?"

"She came to my house. Just showed up."

"Hope you suited up first."

"What? No. We didn't have sex."

"Surprise, surprise."

"She says she's sorry. The last thing she said to me was to tell you that she's really sorry."

"That's why you're here?" Bird said. "To tell me something she could've told me herself?"

"No. I came to see you."

"Because she told you to. And then you almost changed your mind anyway."

"What're you talking about?"

She nodded toward the rack of purses. "How long were you standing there? You came out here, but then the minute you saw me you changed your mind."

"No. You were in the middle of something. And—and, I didn't know what to say."

"Well, you never do, Prettyboy." She re-arranged bottles of perfume on the counter, lining them up and then moving them around again. "You have a good laugh watching me work?"

He lowered his head. The store was as brightly lit as a doctor's office. He wanted to find some shadow to sit down in. "This is why I don't leave the house," he said to no one.

Bird was silent, concentrating on re-arranging the bottles of perfume.

He turned away, then back again. "I'm going to go, then. Good luck with your new career."

"Wait." She raised both hands. "Hold on. OK? Wait a second."

"OK."

She opened a drawer behind her and pulled out a plain, faded denim jacket with dark patches sewn on the elbows. "I'm taking my break," she said to the tall, dark-haired woman at the counter next to her, who didn't look up or respond. Bird slid her arms into the jacket.

Nick said, "Hey, you took off all the pins."

She shrugged. "None of those bands are together anymore. I felt like a dork." She said again, "Nina. I'm going on break."

The woman finally flashed a sullen glance at them. "I heard you the first time."

Bird sighed. "Whatever."

Nick walked alongside her through the aisles. They didn't speak. He'd thought maybe she'd be glad to see him, but now was sure he'd made a mistake. They went out the glass doors and walked along the wide, white sidewalk into a bright, spring day.

Bird said, "So, what the hell happened to your hair?"

"I don't comb it on weekends."

"You're like a hippie now."

"I just need to cut it."

"A haircut's not a lifestyle, dude."

"Well, I don't have a lifestyle either."

She let out a quick laugh.

"What did you do to your teeth?" Nick asked. "They're blinding."

"Smoker's toothpaste. My boss said I couldn't be all smiley and nice to the customers with yellow teeth. I told her I don't smile anyway but she said too bad, it's a job requirement." She sat down on a low brick wall. "This is a good spot. Nobody else takes their break here."

She pulled out a pack of cigarettes and a lighter. Nick sat next to her. The parking lot sprawled out in front of them, filled with cars, afternoon sun glinting off the windshields.

"Look at all the commerce," he said.

"I know." Bird lit her cigarette and pocketed the lighter. "Sometimes, when I leave at night, I'll see one of those cars with that *What Would Jesus Do* sticker or those stupid little fish or that born-again crap." She held her cigarette the way he remembered, like an old-time movie star: pressed between two fingers, palm up, wrist bent back. "If nobody's around, I scrape off the sticker with my razor blade. I'm starting a collection."

Nick watched her as she spoke. Her face seemed more angular now, eyes wider and more prominent. "You look different," he said.

"Nah. It's makeup." She pointed the cigarette at him. "Don't say anything. I have to wear it for work."

"I wasn't going to. You should see how I have to look for work."

"Still doing that office stuff?"

"Yeah. But down in Philly. I take the train every day."

"Just like your old man."

He frowned. "I am not just like my dad."

"If you say so."

She took a long drag, held the smoke for a second, then cast her head back and exhaled a white plume. She coughed. "All right, dude. What's going on with Victoria?"

"Nothing. She's OK."

"Still doing the escort thing?"

"She's quitting."

"Bullshit."

"That's what she told me."

"And you believe it?" Bird's face was tight, mouth a firm line.

Nick shrugged. "Yeah," he said, looking away. "I believe her."

"She's not dying or anything, is she?"

"No. She's fine. Tired. But, fine."

Bird nodded. She rubbed one eye with the back of her hand. "That's cool." Her face softened. Her mouth relaxed.

"Like I told you," he said. "She says she's sorry. But I don't know about what."

She crossed her arms. "Did she tell you why I moved out?"

"Not really."

"Every night I came home from that stupid mailroom job and, if she *was* home, she'd be sitting in the dark just staring out the window. You know what was outside our window? An alley and a brick wall. So what the hell was she seeing? And I know her better than anybody and I knew that look on her face. So every night I'd be unlocking the door to the apartment wondering if I'd have to call 911 and then clean her blood out of the bathtub or something. The days when she was all chatty and happy I'd be wondering, OK, how long is this gonna last? It was like, fucking exhausting."

Nick rubbed his face. He thought about his father, fidgeting in the lobby of the psychiatric center. And his mother, perpetually frowning, a book of crossword puzzles on her lap, sitting in the car outside the therapist's office because she said the other people in the waiting room made her too upset. "I hate the thought you're like any of them," she'd said.

"So, one night, I get home," Bird said. "And there she was at the kitchen table with my razor blades and X-Acto knives all laid out, just staring at them. That was it. I took all that stuff off the table and threw it in my backpack. And she's just sitting, watching me. You know that stare she has—"

"Yeah."

"—it's like when you look up at the sky for too long. You lose perspective. So, she's staring with those, like, snow-blind eyes and you can't tell if she's really seeing you or not and all she can say is 'I'm so stupid, Bird, I don't know what to do.' And I'm like trying to talk to her but that's all she can say, over and over like a tape loop. Like I wasn't even there. So I left. Maybe it was a shitty thing to do, but I walked out. All my clothes fit in one bag. I slung that over my shoulder, grabbed my paintings and split."

Bird shook her head. She pulled her hair back from her face and tucked it behind her ears.

"It *was* a shitty thing to do," she said, staring down at the ground.

"There's nothing else you can do. Or could've done, I mean."

"Yeah, probably." She straightened up and looked around. "So then she calls me for my birthday, like out of nowhere. My throat got all, like, closed up. I couldn't speak."

"She thought you didn't want to talk to her."

"That's not it. After I moved out . . . I don't know."

Nick waited. It was weird to see Bird so hesitant.

"It was like, OK . . ." she said. "I'm back in my fake home with these fake parents. I mean, they're my real parents but totally fake human beings. All that shit that happened to me when I was a kid and they never said one word. And never, well—whatever. Forget about all that. But, like I said, I'm back in the fake house and they're all pretending we're normal like they always do. And I got this job pretending to be all nice and shit to people who are buying all this fake crap—I mean, why the fuck would you call a perfume 'Anais' anyways? So, I'm doing this nicey-nice act with these phonies and their fake shit so they can pretend they're beautiful sex bombs or whatever. And I was, I don't know, not cool with it, but like, well fuck it, whatever. I'll just deal."

"Reconciled to it."

"Yeah. So I'm rolling along on my own fake little trip and then Vicky calls. And my throat just closes up. And she's going, 'what's the deal? What's going on? I miss you,' and I was like: no voice. No words. I didn't even want to *acknowledge* my life. You know what I mean?"

"Oh, yeah."

"Seriously?"

"Yeah. I was on the train yesterday. This is going to sound stupid, but for some reason I was thinking, what would Bird think if she could see me right now?"

She smiled. "Probably be laughing my ass off."

"Probably. But it helps me to think that. It's easy to ignore—no, *deny*—the way your life really is when everybody else you see is doing the exact same thing. You can trick yourself into thinking that's the way it should be. Until something unexpected happens, or like, you wake up and for a moment can't remember where you are, and suddenly you see things differently for a second. Then, you recognize the bullshit for what it is."

"But you're still on the train, just like everybody else. And you'll be on it again tomorrow."

"I know. I'm there, I'm part of it, but this isn't like before. It doesn't touch me the way it used to. I don't get angry or waste time trying to prove that I'm different. That I'm any better." He sighed. "I'm there, yeah. But it's like Victoria says. I'm still here. Still me."

She glanced over his shoulder. Her co-worker, the tall woman in a black dress, stood at the entrance to the mall. She pointed at Bird and threw her hands up in the air.

Bird stood up. "I'm coming!" she shouted. "I still have five minutes!" She sat back down.

"Did you know they closed down the 321?" Nick said.

"Yeah. I stopped going there anyway. Most everybody stopped."

"You still keep up with them?"

"No. I just hear stuff every once in a while. Like, Rachel got married."

"Who?"

"You know. Crow. She married the lead singer in some band from New York. They do that clanky stuff with synthesizers."

"That sucks."

"You liked her?"

"No, I meant about the synthesizers."

She laughed. "It's not Flock of Seagulls shit. More like that German band that makes all that noise."

"Oh. Industrial."

"The music's all right. But it's like something's missing."

"Every new song I hear sounds like it's missing something," Nick said. "I turn on PRB and every song reminds me of one I heard two years ago."

"You think it's us or the music?"

He shrugged. "Every once in a while I'll hear something that'll give me that kick in the chest. That feeling I get from 7 Seconds or Minor Threat."

"Seriously. I crank up my tapes every morning before I come in here. It's the only way I can deal. Those tapes are like my only friends."

"What about Rat? You talk to her?"

"Not much. She tried going to art school, because she figured she'd fit in there. But she didn't get accepted. Probably, cause she can't draw for shit. So she's going to the community college. Land of the lunkheads." She winced. "Not the best place for a little chubby hardcore chick."

They were quiet for a little while.

Nick said, "It's too bad about the 321."

"No, it isn't. It's cool that it's not around anymore."

"Come on. I would have nothing at all if it wasn't for that place."

"That's not what I'm saying. It's more like . . ." She went to speak, hands gesturing, then stopped.

"Is this charades?" he said. "How many guesses do I get?"

"Shut up. I don't have, like, real conversations anymore. It's hard to figure out how to say shit."

"OK. Sorry."

She pursed her lips. "When I was down in Philadelphia, all these posers were telling me 'oh that scene is dead,' 'that's so over.' One guy was even like, 'why are you still listening to Minor Threat? You know Ian's in Fugazi now, right?' No shit! I know that. Does that mean I'm not allowed to listen to Minor Threat anymore? Jesus Christ, all the best bands were touring while we were in fucking junior high. Nobody's as good as they used to be. But it doesn't make the whole thing like, totally *invalid* just because it ended, you know?"

"I know. We caught a lot of good bands."

"I'm not saying it sucked. But I get pissed when people keep saying you missed out. I don't want to hear that shit. Anything that lasts forever is fake. Totally forced." She pointed over one shoulder. "The only thing that'll last forever is this mall. Or this fucking parking lot."

"Or where I work. All those skyscrapers, they'll last forever."

"Right. Like, you hear a really good song on an album and when it ends you think, that *killed.* Then like five seconds of total silence, just the needle crackling, and for that whole five seconds all you're thinking about is, *what's next*? What's the next one going to sound like? So I like things that don't last. It's cool. Because then you can say, 'All right, so what? What's next?' You know what I mean?"

She squinted against the sunlight. It made her look old and serious. Nick felt a deep, airless hollow open up in his chest. He didn't want her to walk away from him again, not like last time.

"You have the goofiest look on your face right now," she said.

"I missed you."

"You're just saying that because you haven't seen me in like a year."

"No. I'm serious. That's why I'm here. I miss you."

She hesitated, lips parted as if to speak, then shook her head.

"What is it?" he asked.

"I can't be around another Victoria. You used to be just like her. In your own dorky way."

"No. I don't feel like that anymore."

"Yeah? How can you tell?"

He was silent for a moment, head bowed. He felt her watching him. Cars meandered up and down the parking lot like lost sheep. "Everything's back to exactly the same as it was before I met all of you. Work, Hopewell, commuting. Everything's the same." He raised his head. He hadn't realized this until just now. "Except, now I know things can be different. I didn't know that before, because I was surrounded by people doing the exact same thing without question, as if we all had a script to follow. But it's possible to do something different. It might not last, it might not work, but so what? There's at least the *possibility* of something besides this." He turned to her. "So, like you said—I want to know what's next."

Bird's cigarette had burned down. She rolled the filter between her fingers, eyes downcast as if in contemplation.

"With you, I mean," he said.

She nodded slowly, then stood and straightened her jacket. She looked around like she'd forgotten where she was. "I'm gonna get crap from those cokeheads for my long break."

"Sorry about that."

She flicked her cigarette butt into the parking lot. "Screw them." She fixed him with her old stare, chin raised. "Are you gonna call me?"

"Yes, Marla. I will."

"Call me Bird. Nobody calls me that anymore."

"OK. Bird."

"You seriously gonna call me?"

"You seriously gonna pick up this time?"

She backed away a few steps. "I don't know."

He smiled. "Then maybe not."

She twisted her mouth in a sneer. "Fuck you," she said, then grinned.

She turned and walked toward the doors. A man and woman passed between them, laden with shopping bags, two red-faced sullen boys in tow, blocking his view for a moment.

"I like your jacket!" Nick shouted.

Without turning, Bird raised both tiny fists in the air and kept walking. Pasted across the back of her denim jacket was a wrinkled anti-abortion sticker that she'd written over in black marker.

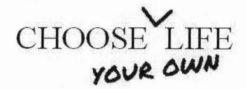

Who cares? That's the last song on the album. . . .

—Hüsker Dü "Plans I Make"

DISCOGRAPHY

The following songs were quoted or referred to in this story (in order of appearance):

"The Order of Death" by Lydon, Levene and Atkins. From: Public Image Limited *This Is What You Want, This Is What You Get* (Elektra/Asylum Records, 1984).

"Institutionalized" by Mike Muir. From: *Suicidal Tendencies* (Frontier Records, 1983).

"Let's Lynch the Landlord" by Jello Biafra. From Dead Kennedys *Fresh Fruit for Rotting Vegetables* (Alternative Tentacles, 1980).

"Can I Say" and "Justification" by Dag Nasty. From: Dag Nasty *Can I Say* (Dischord Records, 1986).

"Back Against the Wall" by The Circle Jerks. From: The Circle Jerks *Group Sex* (Frontier Records, 1980).

"Killing for Jesus" by Bob Ricketts, Eddie Munoz, Harlan Hollander. From: The Circle Jerks *Wonderful* (Combat Core, 1985).

"For Want Of" by Rites of Spring. From: *Rites of Spring* (Dischord Records, 1985).

"Cheer" by The Descendants. From: The Descendants *Enjoy* (SST Records, 1986).

"In Your Face" by Kevin Seconds. From: 7 Seconds *Walk Together Rock Together* (Positive Force, 1984, Better Youth Organization, 1985).

"Terminal Preppie" by Jello Biafra. From: Dead Kennedys *Plastic Surgery Disasters* (Alternative Tentacles, 1982).

"You Look at You" by The Rollins Band. From: The Rollins Band *Life Time* (Texas Hotel, 1988).

"Swinging Man" by H. Rollins, G. Ginn. From: Black Flag *My War* (SST Records, 1983).

"Indecision Time" by Bob Mould. From: Hüsker Dü *Zen Arcade* (SST Records, 1984).

"Kid Dynamite" From: Squirrel Bail *Skag Heaven* (Homestead Records, 1986).

"California Pipeline" by Murphy's Law. From: *Murphy's Law* (Profile Records, 1986).

"American Waste" by Chuck Dukowski. From: Black Flag *The First Four Years* (SST Records, 1984).

"Holidays in the Sun" by Johnny Rotten, Paul Cook, Sid Vicious, Steve Jones. From: *Never Mind the Bollocks Here's the Sex Pistols* (Warner Bros., 1977).

"Life Sentence" by Jello Biafra. From: Dead Kennedys *Give Me Convenience or Give Me Death* (Alternative Tentacles, 1987).

"Wonderful" by Greg Hetson, Keith Clark, Keith Morris. From: Circle Jerks *Wonderful* (Combat Core, 1985).

"Minor Threat" by Minor Threat. From: *Minor Threat* (Dischord Records, 1984).

"The Girl Who Lives on Heaven Hill" by G. Hart. From: Hüsker Dü *New Day Rising* (SST Records, 1985).

"Take the Skinheads Bowling" by Krummenacher, Lowery, Molla, Segal. From: Camper Van Beethoven *Telephone Free Landslide Victory* (Independent Project Records, 1985).

"We're Gonna Fight" by Kevin Seconds. 7 Seconds From: *Walk Together Rock Together* (Positive Force, 1984, Better Youth Organization, 1985).

"Out of Step" by Minor Threat. From: *Minor Threat* (Dischord Records, 1984).

"Moon Over Marin" by East Bay Ray, Jello Biafra. From: Dead Kennedys *Plastic Surgery Disasters* (Alternative Tentacles, 1982).

"Filet of Sole" by The Dead Milkmen. From: The Dead Milkmen *Big Lizard in my Backyard* (Restless Records, 1985).

"Police Story" by Greg Ginn. From: Black Flag *Damaged* (SST Records, 1981).

"Ready to Explode" by J. Keighly. From: D.O.A. *True (North), Strong & Free* (Profile Records, 1987).

"Skinhead Rebel" by Murphy's Law. From: *Murphy's Law* (Profile Records, 1986).

"Where Were You?" by Jon Langford, Tom Greenhalgh. From: The Mekons *Where Were You? Hen's Teeth and Other Lost Fragments of Unpopular Culture (Volume 2)* (Quarterstick Records, 1999).

"Beat My Head Against the Wall" by G. Ginn. From: Black Flag *My War* (SST Records, 1983).

"We Are All Prostitutes" by The Pop Group. (Rough Trade, 1979)

"Chickenshit Conformist" by Jello Biafra. From: *Bedtime for Democracy* (Alternative Tentacles, 1986).

"Plans I Make" by B. Mould, Hüsker Dü. From: Hüsker Dü *New Day Rising* (SST Records, 1985).

The Necros flyer quoted in Chapter 5, "You Look at You" is by Robert Anderson; it can be found in *Fucked Up + Photocopied: Instant Art of the Punk Rock Movement* by Bryan Ray Turcotte and Christopher T. Miller (Gingko Press).

ACKNOWLEDGEMENTS

This story began as an essay about a Circle Jerks concert I wrote for Katharine T. Hoff's writing class at Rider University. My thanks to her for the encouragement and advice, and for rightly pointing out that, as much as I thought I was mimicking Hemingway and Carver, my real models were the songs I'd heard on WPRB and WTSR in the 80's.

Although writing is done in solitude, it is not solitary. My thanks to:

My mother and father for their faith and support, and my Aunt Marie for always sending a card when I needed it most. My compatriots in the Cockeye Book Club, especially Joyce Victor-Chmil, who's read almost every single draft of this (you were right, Joyce). For their critiques, assistance, and encouragement: Mark Dobrowolski, Colleen Ellis, Cristina Lemus, J. Michael Lennon, James Maloney, Matt Maloney, Nancy McKinley, and Richard Swain.

Jaime Hernandez's *Wigwam Bam* and John Porcellino's *Perfect Example* were beside me the entire time I worked on this book. My thanks to these writer/artists for the inspiration and education. My thanks also to Joy Division for their song "Warsaw," which got me through many late nights, and to Simon Reynolds' *Rip It Up and Start Again: Postpunk 1978 – 1984* for asking the right questions.

For a story about a scene that thrived without any corporate backing or influence, and endured on self-reliance and resourcefulness, I can think of no better home than Northampton House Press. My thanks to David Poyer and Lenore Hart, and to Heather Harlen for introducing me to NHP. For making this book so much better: a grateful bow to Lenore for her deadly accurate editing, her vision, and her insight.

This book is a memorial—not for what has died, but for what has passed—so my final grateful acknowledgement is to the bands, the crews, the staff, and the audience members (especially Rebecca) who passed through City Gardens in Trenton, New Jersey, the venue on which the 321 Club is based.

ABOUT THE AUTHOR

Jim Scheers grew up in New Jersey and currently lives in Philadelphia. Over the last three decades he's maintained secret identities such as file clerk, accountant, and technical writer while he focused on his real interest: fiction. Apparently, the secret identities worked almost too well. *This Is What You Want, This Is What You Get* is his first novel.

Northampton House Press

Northampton House publishes carefully selected fiction – historical, romance, thrillers, fantasy, literary—and lifestyle nonfiction, memoir, and poetry. Our mission is to discover great writers and give them a chance to springboard into fame. See our list at www.northampton-house.com, and Like our Facebook page – "Northampton House Press" – for more works of high quality from brilliant new writers.

Made in the USA
Charleston, SC
24 November 2014